JAIME

SINGLE DADS OF GAYNOR BEACH

SA SWAY

CHAPTER 1

JAIME

I sat back as gently as I could, Evie still cradled in my arms. She was fast asleep and as innocent as anything in the universe. She looked peaceful now. She often did. At two months old, she had no way of knowing that her life was already in shambles, starting with her mother and now me.

I looked down at her, the TV playing quietly in the background. I often left it on the random baby shows on the one local network that my antennae could catch. Otherwise, the apartment was too quiet and my thoughts too loud.

Evie was so tiny. So breakable.

When I held her, I wondered if she could feel my fear. Did she know that I was terrified of hurting her accidentally? Anything could. She was so soft and so, *so small*.

Tears pricked the back of my eyes. It kept happening lately out of the blue. My eyes burned, and my chest tightened. Panic rose up my throat.

I didn't move. I couldn't. What if I dropped her?

Suddenly, a sound penetrated my spiraling thoughts—a guitar that started a peaceful strumming.

My eyes flew open as the opening jingle for the local show *Mr. McIntosh* played.

His friendly, smiling face appeared on the screen and immediately soothed something inside of me.

As the show started, I reached for the remote, turning the volume up.

"Hi there, I'm Mr. McIntosh," he said. "And today, I'm very upset. Do you ever feel upset?"

I took a shaking breath, letting his calm voice wash over me.

His show was short and intended for kids up to five years old. He would talk for a minute about various topics like feelings, holidays, and basic everyday things. Sometimes he would read one of his books; sometimes he would sing a song on the guitar. It was simple and relaxing and probably educational. And it was sometimes the only thing that made the world feel sane out there while I was holed up in my basement apartment with an entire human being that relied on me for everything.

"There once was a very naughty puppy named Scruff who got upset sometimes too. He would act out in all sorts of ways when feeling down, but that didn't help to fix things. Would you like to hear his story?" he asked.

He opened his book, and the camera zoomed in. For a moment, I was looking at his clean, surprisingly strong-looking hands on the pages, and then the screen transitioned to the book's first picture, switching to the next as he continued the story.

Somehow, my eyes were drooping by the time he finished reading. When his face was shown again, I

2

couldn't help but snort. In reality, this was a normal man who worked with kids. He was surprisingly masculine for a kid's show host and had an air that reminded me of my friend's dad's growing up—like he knew what was best. He was maybe in his thirties and played the guitar, and probably went out for drinks with friends on weekends.

If he knew that a twenty-three-year-old guy watched his show in a non-ironic way—that it was the only thing that made me feel like I could relax sometimes—he would probably laugh in my face.

I shut my eyes, pushing the thought away. Stopping that shame spiral before it could start.

Mr. McIntosh seemed genuinely too nice for that. As ridiculous as it was to base my opinion of the man on a character he played on TV, I couldn't help feeling it was true.

He was so calm and gentle. I bet that he would know what to do with an infant. He wouldn't spend every night sleeping in the armchair because he was too afraid to lie down and wake the baby up. He wouldn't have heart palpitations every time the baby needed a bath. He would be a good daddy. The kind that Evie deserved. The kind that I never would be.

"Thank you for watching, and remember, if you would like to meet me in person and listen to me read my new book, feel free to drop by Boardwalk Books and Bites on Friday the eleventh at two PM."

I stared at Mr. McIntosh's gentle, dimpled smile, his slightly crooked nose, and kind blue eyes as the screen faded to the details of his next reading.

Two days from now…

I couldn't go. I wouldn't be able to talk to him.

My hands started to shake just thinking about it, but then… hearing his voice in person, seeing him in the flesh…

How could I not?

CHAPTER 2

ETHAN

I COMBED MY HANDS THROUGH MY HAIR, SWEEPING THE DUSKY blond locks into shape. I hadn't had time to shave this morning, but hopefully a bit of stubble wouldn't ruin the illusion for the children.

"You received another call from Evan," Naomi said.

I glanced over at my assistant, not surprised to see the knowing look on her face.

"Should I tell him you'll call?" she asked.

Evan was okay. He was relatively upbeat and fun, but he was pushy too... He was a bartender at The Cantina and seemed to love that lifestyle of staying up late, drinking a lot, always on the lookout for fun. I wasn't opposed to a good time, but I worked with children and we filmed early on weekdays. The sex had been decent, but even in bed, he was a bit too bossy for my tastes. Basically, we had very little in common. I wasn't quite sure why I'd gone on two dates with him, except maybe out of boredom. Now, two weeks later, he was still hounding Naomi whenever I said I was busy, trying to get her to find time to squeeze him in. I really should have told him I wasn't interested, but I was just so over having those conversations with guys. There didn't seem to be anyone able to keep my attention for more than a couple of hours anymore.

"Just tell him I'm busy," I sighed. "I'll call him back later."

Naomi nodded, quickly typing out a message on her phone. As she did, I turned my attention back to the mirror, adjusting my tie one last time.

A lot of thought had gone into Mr. McIntosh, right down to the wardrobe. Did I want him to feel like a friend, a confidant, a neighbor? In the end, I'd gone with a friendly teacher persona. I always wore a button-down and a tie in soft colors. I was always neat and clean. I was often told how friendly and welcoming I seemed on the show and took it as a deep compliment. Working with kids wasn't for everyone, but I loved every moment of it. Even on the days when I was tired, or reading the same story for the hundredth time, the thought of making a difference in anyone's life made it worth it.

"He says he's going to come by later," Naomi said.

I groaned.

"To my place?" I asked.

She nodded, grimacing, and held up the phone to show me the messages. I read them quickly, annoyance rising. Her polite *Mr. Mack is busy for the day* was answered with *No worries, I'll drop by his place tonight at seven.*

"See?" I said, sighing. "*Pushy.*"

She bit back a grin.

"He's into you. I wish hot guys threw themselves at me too. I definitely wouldn't be brushing them off as often as you do."

I chuckled. Naomi was pretty, with a black bob and

striking green eyes. People gave her plenty of attention, but her standards were extremely high, so I felt no pity when she complained.

"Fine. Tell him that works… I'll probably still cancel on him before he comes over though."

"Yeah, yeah."

She typed a quick message, then went to the doorway, peeking into the main room of the bookshop. It was big and we were in the office, which was on the opposite corner of the reading area. I didn't know how much she could see, but she leaned back into the room with wide eyes.

"It's busy out there. Should I go out and get them all ready?"

I nodded.

"I'm good when you are."

Naomi grinned, gave me a thumbs up, and stepped out.

A minute later, as the door drifted shut, I heard her usual speech begin.

"Hello! Welcome, everyone! If you could take your seats, Mr. McIntosh is almost ready to begin. Are you ready to hear a great story?"

The door sealed shut but I went to it, still listening, smiling at the enthusiastic way she spoke to the crowd.

With the door shut, I could barely hear her.

As always, my heart started to pound a little with nerves. It would go away once I started the reading, but I couldn't help feeling a little anxious every time. It still took getting used to having so many eyes trained on me. More than that, though, reading a new book to a group was always a bit daunting. Would the kids like it as much as they had liked the other ones? Would the parents? Would they ask the right questions and give the reactions that I hoped for?

When it came to kids in the age group I focused on—basically toddlers to pre-K—you had to be prepared for anything. One of my earliest readings had ended with me shutting the book halfway through to help wrangle all the excited children. And at the end, I'd laughed along with the parents and played my guitar so the little ones had something to dance to. Though hectic at the time, it was one of my favorite memories and always made me smile. Thinking of it now, all the nerves faded into the background to be replaced with excitement.

I really hoped they liked Rowdy the Frog as much as my editor and publisher did, but seeing the kids was more important.

"Put your hands together to welcome Mr. McIntosh!"

At the sound of the light applause, my smile grew. Toddlers didn't usually grasp the applause system, which meant the parents had to clap louder. It was sweet but unnecessary. I'd told Naomi to stop making people clap. When I read at the library, Mikaela, the assistant there, always did it too.

Oh well. I appreciated the gesture and stepped into the bookstore, still smiling.

My steps faltered a little when I saw how many people filled the space. The shop was packed this time. Children crowded the floor at the front, all the way up to the seat I was supposed to sit on. Every audience chair was full, with either a parent on their own or holding a young child. A couple of them had quiet babies strapped to their chests. Behind them, more people were standing, filing between the shelves.

"Wow," I said, coming to my spot in front of the

display stand, feeling the heat of so many bodies. "I feel like I need a microphone."

A couple of people laughed.

I took a moment to look at them all. So many smiling faces.

Warmth bloomed in my chest.

Arty, my producer, had said that our numbers were way up lately. It seemed that he was right.

"Thank you all so much for coming," I said. "I appreciate you choosing to spend your afternoon with me."

I looked down at the kids as I took my seat.

"Are you excited to hear a new story?" I asked.

A couple of them started talking at once. With a trained ear, I was able to answer them both despite them talking over each other.

I told the first child I was delighted to meet him in person after his proclamation that he watched me on TV. For the second child's question about what story we would be reading, I picked up the book and showed it to the audience.

"Today, I'm going to be reading you my newest book, Rowdy the Frog. It's about a frog who gets... can you guess?"

A couple of the kids started to stand, jumping up and down to get my attention.

"Rowdy!" one of them shouted.

I laughed.

"That's right. Have you ever felt rowdy? That means noisy and all over the place. A little wild. Yes, like that," I said as the kids started to act it out.

"Now, let's all have a seat and find out what happens to Rowdy."

To my surprise, the kids all sat down at once, eager to

hear my story. I opened it up to the first page and the illustration there, smiling at the wide-eyed faces. They were all so damn cute.

As I started to read, the room fell silent, everybody hanging on my every word. I paused whenever I could to ask the children questions, making sure they could all understand, but they were quick to get back into it whenever I started to read again.

Around the room, the parents listened aptly. They always did to make sure that it was the right kind of story for their little ones. They were really the people I was selling to after all. But that wasn't what was important to me. What mattered the most were the kids. My eyes flicked across the room again, making sure that no one was being left out. Sometimes the kids in the back felt excluded. But it wasn't a child that caught my eye.

For a moment my gaze landed on a young man at the back of the room, and my words faltered. I didn't know how I hadn't seen him there. He stood out like a sore thumb: a black cloud in the middle of all the happy people. Dark brown hair and eyes, a leather jacket, and a frown complemented the gloomy persona.

What the heck is someone like that doing here? I wondered.

I tore my gaze away, seamlessly moving back to the words in the story, but something kept drawing my eyes back to him.

The way he was looking at me, his eyes boring straight through me, made it hard to speak each time our gazes met. But there was something else, and, as I reached the last pages of the book, I realized with a sudden sinking feeling what it was—a baby. It wasn't in a stroller or carrier of any kind. It was just held in the fold of his jacket. I could only tell it was there by the way he was holding his arm around the bundle. He was clearly being careful. A familiar feeling of loss washed over me.

Anyone looking so depressed while holding an infant was cause for concern in my books. That wasn't my area of expertise though. I was here for the older children. The ones who could follow along and play games, and I definitely wasn't here for their parents...

Yet, no matter how much I told myself that, my eyes kept going to his somber form.

I finished the story and began asking the kids simple comprehension questions as well as some fun ones, like how they would jump if they were Rowdy. The whole room devolved into frog jumps and laughter.

When I looked up again, the man in the back was looking at the floor, seemingly absent from the goings-on. Again, I wondered why he had come.

I stood and began my rounds, taking time for all the parents and children who wanted a moment to talk to me.

Without realizing it, I was working my way across the room toward him.

He didn't notice me coming. Just as well, since I had no idea what I even wanted to say to him, if anything. Only my curiosity wouldn't allow me to leave it.

As I got closer, seeing in more detail the forlorn look on his face, I found myself hoping it wasn't a baby he was holding at all.

His eyes were still glued to the floor when I reached him, and so utterly *sad*. And tired. He didn't look up, didn't even seem to notice me, so I forced a casual remark, attempting to keep my voice light.

"What have you got there?"

I may as well have shot him, the way he jumped.

His wide, doe eyes landed on me like I was a ghost,

and immediately a baby's scream tore through the air.

He looked down, gasping as the small baby started to thrash in his jacket, kicking small, pink-socked feet free.

"Sh, sorry, baby," he muttered, bouncing her, his gaze shooting to mine in panic.

"Let me see?" I asked, instinctively stepping closer.

His breath caught as I reached for the baby, but he carefully extracted her from his jacket and passed her into my arms.

My breath caught at the sight of her.

She was so small—only a couple months old at most. She was in a cute pink onesie, kicking and reaching in that wild infant way.

I forced a smile, calming my voice.

"Hello sweetheart," I said, "did you get startled?"

I lifted her to my shoulder and patted her back gently while I rocked her.

"There, there."

To my relief, she calmed down almost at once.

Her father—or guardian or whoever he was—was biting his lips, watching. When she stopped crying, a gentle smile pulled his lips.

"She's looking around," he said, as though surprised and my unease grew.

"Is she yours?" I asked.

He nodded, swallowing.

"Yeah, this is Evie."

He couldn't quite look at me, his gaze focused on his little girl. He reached out, rubbing her back gently.

"This is the bookstore," he said to her. "Do you like it?"

She made a gurgling sound, and his smile grew, gaze flickering to mine for only a moment—almost shyly. "This is Mr. McIntosh," he said to Evie. "From the TV."

My stomach swooped unexpectedly. Why was it the textbook bad boys who always had those sweet, charming smiles? This guy's lips, full and pouty, looked even better curved up like that.

I swallowed.

"So, does Evie watch my show?" I asked.

The smile dropped off his face, replaced with embarrassment.

"It feels weird watching adult stuff with her there," he said. "I just keep kid's shows on."

There was no need to explain, but Evie definitely wasn't the one watching my show. He had brought her here because, for whatever reason, he had wanted to see me. That much was clear.

"That makes sense," I said though, and he looked up at me then, facing me properly. God, he was attractive... and the way he was looking at me... If he didn't stop, it was going to go straight to my head. "I got Evie's name, but what is yours?"

"Uh—Jaime."

He offered a hand. I had to shift Evie around before I could give him mine. His hand was warm and strong when our palms met.

"Nice to meet you Jaime, I'm Ethan."

He gaped.

"Oh. Right. Ethan."

He seemed shocked that I had a regular name. To be honest, even I was surprised that I had given it. At events like these, I was Mr. McIntosh. I didn't want to ruin the illusion for the children. Realizing what I had done, I glanced around. No one was standing close enough to hear us. There were still some kids running around and others were standing around and talking, but the crowd had thinned considerably. I was touched to see that the display of Rowdy the Frog books had been nearly emptied. A few kids sat on the floor in front of it, rereading the story.

Naomi was standing by my chair at the other end. As soon as our eyes met, she waved me over.

My heart felt full at the same time that a deep, anxious feeling swept through me. I wasn't ready to walk away. The idea of giving Evie back to Jaime made my heart start racing.

With a slow, steady breath, I handed her over.

Jaime took her carefully, cradling her like she was made of glass.

"Do you need a carrier?" I asked. "I have one you can take."

The words just popped out of my mouth. It was an utter lie and completely crossed a line. I didn't know these people. It wasn't my job to get involved, but when Jaime nodded hesitantly, relief filled me.

"I don't have one," he said. "But it's fine—"

"No, really, I have no need for it. Can I give it to you?"

He swallowed and nodded.

"Um. Yeah. Okay."

Naomi was suddenly at my side.

"Hey, Mr. McIntosh, we have to clear out now. I think Nash wants his bookstore back."

I followed her gaze, seeing the owner coming toward us with a smile and thumbs up.

I grinned, waved, and turned hastily back to Jaime, eager to get his number before we were interrupted.

I fished my phone out of my pocket and handed it to him.

"Call your number?"

He took it, his face swiftly turning pink as he dialed, just as Nash reached us.

"Looks like another bestseller," he said clapping me on the shoulder.

I shook my head.

"We'll see."

My phone was suddenly pressed to my hand. I took it, catching Jaime as he was backing awkwardly away.

"Bye," he muttered and took off through the shelves before anything else could be said to him.

When I turned back, both Naomi and Nash had the same amused expression on their faces, brows raised.

"Don't tell me you were picking up at a reading?" Nash teased.

I snorted, even as my stomach swooped.

"Please. He was just a fan."

"Ah. A fan. I forgot that you always give your number to fans," Naomi mused.

I groaned.

"It wasn't that."

"Glad to hear," Naomi said. "He gives off stalker vibes."

"Come on, let's pack up," I said, choosing to end the conversation there.

Considering that he'd seemed out of place to me too, I couldn't really argue that. Didn't mean I liked hearing it though. Jaime didn't seem like a bad guy. He couldn't have such a sweet smile if he was.

I forced myself not to look at my phone until we were all ready to go, then pulled it out and quickly checked recent calls. To my relief, there was a new number there.

I smiled softly, then caught myself and swallowed.

What the hell was I doing?

CHAPTER 3

JAIME

I felt weirdly out of sorts. Like everything was upside down.

I hadn't thought about whether Mr. McIntosh—or *Ethan*—would be taller than me. He was, by a solid four inches, with eyes sharper than I'd expected. They were gentle and kind, just like I'd known they would be, but when he looked straight at me, it was intense and unnerving. It felt like he could read my mind. Like I was one of his books, preschool-level complexity and all. All of five minutes required to know everything I was trying to hide.

I swallowed and looked down at Evie. She'd looked so damn perfect over his shoulder, happy and curious and sweet.

For a few minutes after I'd left the bookstore, I'd taken advantage of it, holding her in such a way that she could see the cars passing while we waited for the bus. She fell asleep almost straight away though. For some reason, being out and in my arms made her pass out more than when we were at home and I tried to make her fall asleep.

The bouncing of the bus added to the effect. She was out cold again, drooling and all.

I still couldn't believe that Mr. McIntosh had spoken to us. *Ethan!* That was going to take some getting used to—or not. What was the likelihood that he would actually call me? Especially just to give me something? There was no need. He didn't know me. He didn't owe me anything. He shouldn't call.

But what if he did?

My stomach squirmed with nerves. My heart sped up. Heat rose up my cheeks. It felt like the start of a panic attack but *good.*

I swallowed. I wanted that message or, even better, a call.

Tonight, when I was sitting with Evie asleep in my arms, maybe he would speak to me with that nice voice of his for long enough that I'd drop into sleep myself.

Getting his attention at all, already felt like winning. I was totally unworthy, but hell, it made me feel good.

How heartwarming to learn that someone you admired on TV wasn't a total dickwad and was, in fact, quite friendly.

Realistically, I knew he probably wasn't going to actually message me. I was sure that he was too busy, but the gesture meant a lot.

Arriving at the bookstore, with my heart in my stomach, I'd nearly turned around at the door. Inside, it was hard to ignore how out of place I was. I didn't look like the other parents. Sure, some of them looked tired or worn, the way that I felt, but most of them just looked so... *put together.* It was another blow. More proof that I shouldn't be in this position. That Evie deserved better.

I pressed that thought down, burying it as best I could,

but I could still feel it festering just under the surface. Same way it always did.

Mr. McIntosh, being kind and observant and good with kids, had immediately noticed. He'd pointed it out—albeit in a kind way—that I didn't even have a carrier. He'd known that I was lacking the basic things that she needed.

Now, as distance grew between me and the bookstore and Ethan, as the excitement at meeting him began to wear off, humiliation swept in to take its place.

I was so fucking embarrassed. I'd *known* not to go today...

Groaning, I dropped my head back, letting it hit the rattling window. But at the same time, he had been so nice...

My flip-flopping emotions got me through the bus trip, distracting me enough that I ended up missing my stop. Luckily, I only had to walk an extra five minutes to get home.

The upstairs neighbors, Mr. and Mrs. Woo, were on the front porch. As the homeowners of the small house I lived in, in Oakdale, they'd been delighted with me at first. I'd paid a year upfront and was generally quiet. Then I'd moved Evie in and having to explain the situation to them had been one of the most awkward conversations that I'd had.

Every time she cried since I'd brought her home a month ago, I cringed.

I waved, faking a friendly smile as I passed toward the back door, moving fast enough that I hoped they didn't have a chance to stop me.

No luck, though.

"Jaime! How are you?"

I slowed, turning back to see them.

Mrs. Woo had moved to the edge of the porch and was watching me with the worried face that now seemed to be a permanent fixture whenever she saw me.

"How is everything?" she asked. "Is the baby okay?"

I forced my polite smile to remain intact.

"She's still alive, if that's what you mean?"

"Okay," she said slowly, frown still in place.

I couldn't read this damn woman. All I knew for sure was that the way she and her husband looked at me always made me feel judged and like I wasn't good enough.

"We hear her crying all the time," Mr. Woo piped in.

I felt myself shrink. Evie must have felt my heart drop, pressed against it as she was, because she chose that moment to wiggle and let out a distressed cry.

"Aw," Mrs. Woo said, "can I see her?"

I shook my head, already backing away.

"It's a bit chilly. I need to get her inside."

I hurried to my entrance at the back, quickly unlocking the door and slamming it behind me like I was being chased.

My heart was racing and the jostling had made Evie start to thrash. Her cries rang loud and clear, and in the silence of the basement apartment we lived in, it sounded even louder.

I carefully withdrew her from the warmth of my jacket and hurried to the bedroom, placing her carefully on her back in the center of the bed where I could watch her while I pulled off my jacket.

"You hungry, sweetheart?" I asked and bent over her, waiting for her to notice me. She didn't though. She was distracted by the current meltdown, her eyes squeezed shut as she kicked aimlessly.

I stroked back the blond fuzz on top of her head, wondering if I could leave her there for a moment while I warmed her bottle.

She would be okay. She couldn't even roll over yet.

I made it to the door before anxiety hit me hard and the thought *what if*. What if she did somehow roll over? What if the blankets smothered her?

I was back at her side, lifting her up while my heart pounded as though I'd literally just saved her from imminent death.

What the hell?

Taking a shuddering breath, I lifted her onto my shoulder, trying to channel Ethan's calm energy and confidence.

It didn't help at all. The entire time the water was boiling and the bottle was warming, she screamed in my ear.

When I finally settled with her in my arms on the armchair she seemed to like, right in front of the TV with the bottle in her mouth, my nerves were on edge. I didn't turn on the TV. I couldn't handle any extra noise. The sound of Evie drinking soothed me a little bit, but when my phone vibrated, I jumped.

I had to wiggle a bit to get to it without disrupting her feeding, but I somehow pulled it out of my pocket without taking the bottle out of her mouth.

Ethan's face flashed in my mind, but I stomped that flickering hope down. I didn't know who it could be. My friends had dropped off the face of the earth once I had a child. It didn't help that I'd already drawn back when I got sick of all the partying.

Evie wasn't to blame. She'd just sped up the process, but the sudden isolation hadn't helped matters.

I flicked on my phone and stared in confusion for a minute.

The number wasn't in my contacts, but the message I'd received said it all.

> Hi Jaime. This is Ethan Mack. It was nice to meet you today. Any chance you can drop me your address? I want to swing by with my spare carrier.

I stared for so long that I didn't even notice Evie had stopped drinking and fallen back to sleep until milk was pouring onto my arm.

Cursing, I pulled the bottle away and set it on the side table. I wiped the spilled milk with my other sleeve, keeping her where she was as I read the message again. Finally, I typed my address and hit send.

As an afterthought, I added a *thank you*.

His message was polite. He wasn't trying to be friends or anything and that was okay. I was still in shock and even touched that he was really carrying through with the offer. It wasn't what I'd expected.

Since Liz had deposited Evie into my life and left, I hadn't had anyone even check in. I'd learned a long time ago that people didn't do that.

Something inside me stirred. A warmth filled me, intensifying when I received Ethan's next message.

> Be there in fifteen minutes.

CHAPTER 4

ETHAN

I PULLED UP IN FRONT OF THE HOUSE, RELIEVED TO SEE THAT the neighborhood looked nice enough. The house was a modest but neat place, that was clearly cared for.

Just seeing it eased the concern that had been eating away at me since the reading today. They lived in a normal house. He was probably too young to be in there alone. Maybe there was a mother on the scene or family members.

With that bit of relief, I climbed the front steps, brand new carrier in hand, and knocked on the door.

To my surprise, an elderly Asian woman answered the door.

For a moment, we blinked at each other blankly.

"Oh, hi there," I said, smiling. "I seem to have the wrong address. I was looking for someone named Jaime."

I leaned back, trying to see the number again.

"Oh, yes, Jaime lives downstairs," she said. "Back door."

"Ah. Okay, thanks."

She nodded and shut the door as that light feeling slowly sank back down.

Basement suite? I guessed, climbing down the steps and going around the side of the house.

A door with chipped blue paint was set against the wall but down a few steps.

Even on this relatively warm spring day, the cement was damp and wet.

I braced myself and knocked.

It only took a moment for Jaime to open the door. I tried to hide my disappointment as I saw the darkness of his apartment behind him.

Jaime had lost the leather jacket and was in a black t-shirt now. Tattoos snaked around his forearms and his brown hair was a mess, as though he couldn't keep his hands out of it. Evie was still in his arms; his forearms were flexed as though he'd never even put her down... and he was looking even more nervous than he had at the reading. Despite looking like a picture-perfect bad boy, there was something about Jaime that made me want to wrap him up in a blanket and cuddle him.

I forced a smile.

"Hi," I said, holding up the baby carrier.

He blinked at it, brows rising before his gaze turned back to my eyes, touched with something like wonder.

"Wow," he muttered, "you really came."

"Why wouldn't I?" I asked, offering it to him.

He shook his head.

"Sorry."

He reached out, taking the carrier. He looked at it for a moment, then let it fall to his side.

"This will be really helpful," he said. "Thanks again."

I nodded.

"No worries... You need a hand figuring it out?"

He swallowed.

"I'm sure I can manage."

That was my cue to leave, but what Jaime didn't know, what I had barely even acknowledged, was that I wasn't just here to give it to him. I was here to see his home, to see the way he was living. and now that I was faced with that fact, I was going to push for it.

"I don't mind," I said, offering a smile and gently tugging the carrier back. "Can I come in?"

He stared at me for a long moment and then moved out of the doorway.

"Uh. Sure."

I stepped into the darkness that was Jaime's apartment, taking it all in at once.

The basement was finished, but it still felt like a basement. The windows were small and too close to the ceiling to easily look through. The floors were covered in a worn, cream carpet.

We were standing right in the living room. The kitchen was visible through the arch next to me. What looked like a small hall must have led to the washroom and bedroom.

"Um. Can I get you something?" Jaime asked from behind me.

I turned to him. He was biting his full bottom lip, looking up at me.

I knew I shouldn't prolong this visit. Then again, I wasn't supposed to be here, to begin with.

"Sure," I said. "What do you have?"

"Coffee?" he asked. "Or water or tea?"

"Coffee would be great."

He gave me a small, guarded smile, walking into the kitchen ahead of me.

I watched as he started to fill the pot with water with one hand, his back to me. As expected, he didn't seem to have anywhere to put Evie down.

"Here," I said, touching his arm.

He nearly jumped out of his skin, spinning to look at me.

I kept my face carefully neutral.

"I can hold Evie while you do that."

He took a calming breath.

"Oh. Yeah, okay."

With utmost care, he passed her snoozing form into my arms.

She didn't wake up, so I settled into a seat at the table, mind spinning while I watched him move around the kitchen and listened to the sound of her soft breathing.

"How do you get anything done?" I blurted.

Jaime paused, glancing at me over his shoulder.

"What do you mean?"

"You're always holding her, right?" I asked.

"She's light," he said, shrugging.

Pressing the button on the machine, he turned and leaned his hips against the counter, his gaze falling on Evie.

A soft smile touched his face.

"She looks so peaceful with you," he said.

My heart squeezed.

"She looks peaceful with you too," I informed him, and his brown eyes shot to mine.

"Does she really?" he asked.

"Yeah, of course," I said at once. "You can tell she is very comfortable with her daddy."

Jaime's smile grew. It was filled with hope and fear all

at once, and my stomach continued to drop all the way to my ankles.

"You know you're doing a good job, don't you?" I couldn't help asking and my voice suddenly started to tremble, because I was finally saying those words out loud to someone who needed them. I'd lost countless nights of sleep wondering if they would have made a difference had they been said to my mother.

I swallowed the lump in my throat as I watched all the emotions flickering across Jaime's face. Finally, his expression settled into a frown, and he turned around abruptly, pulling mugs out of the cupboard.

The coffee splashed over the edges of both cups when he started pouring.

"Milk?" he asked in a trembling voice.

"Yes," I said, watching as he spilled a bit of that too.

Finally, he set the carton down, took a deep breath, calmly wiped the counter, and turned back to face me, coffees in hand.

He set one in front of me and took the seat across from me, sipping quietly, all while avoiding eye-contact.

That suited me just fine. It meant I could stare.

Jaime was incredibly beautiful. The more I looked at him, the more it hit me. He was like a wildflower, thorns and edges and bright emotions, just as ready to fight as he was to wilt and break.

"How old are you?" I found myself asking.

"Twenty-three," he muttered, finally risking a quick glance at me. "Why? Too young to take good care of her?"

I shook my head at once, fighting the rising tension. So, Jaime liked to pick fights when he was upset. I had plenty of experience dealing with that gut reaction from people, especially after years of social work. Everyone wanted to defend themselves however they could, but I wouldn't fall for the bait.

"Not at all. I've known younger parents than you who were wonderful to their kids. And Evie obviously trusts you, even at, what, two or three months?"

"Two," he said softly.

His fingers played over the chipped flower design on his mug.

"Do you really think she likes me?" he asked in a small voice. "How can you tell?"

I managed a small smile even as my heart squeezed.

"Just a hunch. Some babies cry and cry, or they won't sleep at all. She's very easygoing."

He chuckled darkly.

"Well, she'll only sleep if I'm holding her," he admitted.

"All night?" I asked.

He nodded, cheeks turning pink.

"All night. I have to stay up with her."

I took a sip of my coffee, trying to hide my reaction. That was a very bad sign. In terms of mental health, sleep was essential. And he already seemed to be overwhelmed to begin with.

"Does anyone else take a turn?" I asked, fishing for info. "Maybe her mother?"

"No," he said, dark gaze falling to his coffee.

For a while, I didn't think he was going to elaborate. When he looked up at me, with bright, worried eyes, it was like he'd decided *to hell with it*. He was letting it all out.

"Liz is completely out of the picture. I don't know if she's coming back to take Evie but I—I'll fight her. I'll do anything I have to. She can't have Evie back unless she's completely clean. Even then, I don't think I'll ever be able to trust her again."

"Okay," I said slowly, trying to gather my thoughts before I allowed emotion to take over. "That doesn't sound good. She's your child though, right? So, unless Liz is in the best possible state, you'll be given custody. Especially after stepping up the way that you have."

My reassurance seemed to have the opposite effect. His hands started to shake; tears sprang to his eyes and he blinked them back rapidly.

"Shit," he muttered. "No, she's not really mine. Liz is my sister..."

He swallowed, hands clutching his coffee mug until they turned white.

"She showed up here out of the blue with her. I mean, I'd already been thinking about it. I wanted to—I don't know. I've already tried with Liz, but she doesn't listen to me. She doesn't listen to anyone. I wanted to help my niece somehow. Then Liz came here and gave me Evie one night and I just took her."

I stared.

"Wow," I breathed. "That—that's a lot, Jaime. It would be for anyone."

He took a shuddering breath.

"Not for you," he argued.

I shook my head.

"No, Jaime. I would find that to be a big adjustment too."

"Really?" he asked, and he looked so small suddenly, so vulnerable, that I wanted to hold him.

The desire to cross the table and pull the young man into my arms hit me hard.

If not for Evie still in my arms, I would have found it hard to resist.

"Do you have anyone to help?" I asked.

He shook his head.

"Well then... Good thing I'm here," I found myself saying.

It was so wrong on so many levels. I shouldn't be stepping in. I wasn't doing it for the right reasons. Admittedly, part of me was sitting here because of those big brown eyes. The way he looked at me seemed to go straight through me, and I hadn't felt anything like that in a long time. But he was young. And so vulnerable. He needed someone badly. I just worried about that someone being *me*.

I didn't have the best history with newborns. Seeing them ate away at me, especially little girls like Evie, with the pink onesies and baby blond wisps of hair.

But when Jaime shook his head and started to argue, I found myself arguing right back.

"Please," I said. "I wouldn't be able to sleep at night without at least making sure you're both okay. Now that I'm here, I can't just walk away."

I meant that too.

It felt like I was glued to the seat and it would be nearly impossible to pass Evie back to Jaime if I didn't know I could come back to check on them.

Jaime bit his lip, looking at me through those thick, dark lashes, before nodding.

I smiled as my stomach twisted with nerves.

I didn't remember the last time I had felt so conflicted.

CHAPTER 5

JAIME

It felt like a whirlwind, the way Ethan seemed to be flying into my life. I hadn't expected anything from him or *anyone*, yet here he was, insisting. When he set down his coffee and rose to his feet, I followed, allowing him to explore my apartment as I trailed after him.

"There's no bath," he said. "How do you wash her?"

"In the sink," I said, flushing. "The way my mom used to do it."

He nodded like that wasn't the wrong thing to do, and some of my shame eased.

"That's fine," he said. "Might be a bit easier on you if you don't have to hold her though. Until she can sit up at least."

Evie was awake again, her chin perched on Ethan's shoulder while he made notes on his phone.

"Hello Evie," I crooned, brushing my fingers against her arm for comfort really—which was odd, I supposed since she was an infant, but I felt out of my depth and scared and she was the only person here that I knew.

Maybe intrinsically, she could feel that, because she

reached out and snatched my finger in hers with that incredible baby grip, not letting me go.

I couldn't hold back the smile as I was literally pulled through the hall to the bedroom.

Ethan stopped in the doorway, looking around the space for a very long minute without saying anything. I was behind him, so I couldn't read his expression, but when I glanced over his shoulder, everything looked the same as usual. The bed was made, and the drawers were all shut. Dirty clothes were piled in a basket under the window, but everything was clean. The one picture on the wall, a painting of horses galloping, that I had taken from home when I'd first moved—the only thing I had left from my old life was collecting dust on the wall. I didn't think that was what had caught his attention though.

"What is it?" I finally asked.

He turned to look at me over the wrong shoulder, making my arm go around him as my finger was still clasped in Evie's hand and then chuckled and turned around the other way.

"Your room just looks very unused," he finally said. "Where do you put Evie when you go to sleep? Next to you?"

I shook my head.

"No. I told you, she only lets me sleep if I'm holding her."

"Not in bed?"

"On the armchair," I explained.

His brows shot up.

"Okay, let's fix that first. You're raising a child. You deserve to have a solid night's sleep in your own bed."

That did sound nice. Impossible, but nice. Evie wasn't just going to let me sleep without her though. I had tried.

Still, I didn't argue. If anyone could get her to sleep on her own, it was Ethan. He was some kind of baby whisperer for sure, and I knew barely anything except the basics of keeping her alive. I would follow his lead in this and, to be honest, in anything else he wanted to instruct me on. Being in any way as collected and put together as the older man was now a key fantasy for me. To be successful and stable just seemed like the ultimate goal now. Not partying, not friends, just a reliable income, maybe a house, and Evie, healthy and happy...

I shook the images away, surprised at where my thoughts had gone. I hadn't thought about our future before. I'd been so caught up in surviving each moment. The idea of having Evie grow up strong and healthy and happy, basically the complete opposite of how me and my sister had grown up, was both heartwarming and terrifying, because now that I'd thought of it, I was in a mild panic about losing the opportunity.

I took a steadying breath, concentrating on her little hand, still holding mine. She always helped me calm down, even though she was also the source of most of my anxiety. Every day she put me into at least one panic about dropping her or hurting her in some way, and then she would soothe me with those wide eyes and grabby hands... Loving her was like getting whiplash.

"Since I don't have a car seat, we can get to the shop on the bus," Ethan was saying, drawing my attention back to the moment. "Unless you drive?"

I shook my head.

"Uh. No. I know I should. I just—"

—was terrified of being on the road, in control of a vehicle going at speeds that couldn't stop fast enough—

"It's fine, where's the nearest bus stop?"

"Just across the street," I said, still trying to think back to what he had said. "I'm sorry, where are we going?"

"West Coast Snuggles," Ethan said. "To get a crib or bassinet."

I winced.

"Ah, no, that's okay—"

"It's on me," he said at once, but that only made me feel worse.

I stood there, trying to decide how to argue but my mind was blank.

"Everything else, we'll get secondhand, okay? I want you to be able to put her down sometimes though, starting today."

I swallowed and forced myself to nod.

Mr. McIntosh knows best, I told myself. *If he wants to spend his money on me, that's his choice.*

It still felt weird. Mr. McIntosh. Considering that seeing him had left me starstruck just this morning, I thought I was handling this pretty well.

"Want to try this on?" he asked, lifting the baby carrier.

I nodded, taking it.

It didn't look like so many straps could possibly be needed, but before I could figure it out on my own, Ethan reached out, lifting one part and slipping it over my shoulder.

He did the same on the other side, then connected them to the front before moving behind me and attaching it all together.

"It needs to be tight," he said, pulling the straps until it was snug, but I could barely concentrate on anything but the smell of his cologne. It wasn't overpowering, but it seemed to blanket me when he was standing so close. So warm and masculine, just like him. I shut my eyes for a moment and when I opened them again, he was standing in front of me, offering Evie.

I blinked, shaking myself.

"Sorry," I muttered. "Just tired."

He smiled, but there was worry in his eyes.

"That's why we're doing this. You need to be cared for too."

Emotion threatened to overwhelm me at the statement.

I couldn't look at him, so I forced myself to concentrate on putting Evie in safely. Then I looked up at Ethan in wonder.

"It's like she's not even there!" I said, amazed. "She feels so much lighter!"

He grinned.

"Yes! And you have your hands again!"

I laughed, flexing my fingers.

"I'm not used to that anymore."

I looked down at Evie, who was facing in toward me and looking up at the ceiling with newfound interest, looking as comfortable as ever.

"What do you think, baby?"

She gurgled.

"I'll take that as approval."

"Does she have any shoes?" Ethan asked.

"Shoes?" I asked, confused. "She doesn't walk."

He smiled, a real one this time, the corners of his eyes wrinkling.

"I know. It's just to keep her feet warm."

"Oh. No, but she has socks. Liz dropped her off with a bag of stuff. It's over there."

For simplicity, I'd kept her belongings in the bag in the living room where it was all easily accessible. Aside from diapers and bath supplies, I hadn't needed to add to them yet. But maybe there were things she needed that I was unaware of, like shoes.

I watched as Ethan pulled a pair of pink socks onto her tiny feet. Once she was ready, I pulled my jacket on. As always, I tucked a bottle into one pocket and a diaper and travel pack of wipes in the other. Then, I zipped her inside up to the neck so she could still see the sky.

I couldn't stop staring at her.

She looked so happy. And so much more alert too, looking around at the lights on the bus, at the blue sky above. When we reached the shop Ethan had been talking about, West Coast Snuggles, she was blown away by all the signs and colors.

Although we'd only come for a bassinet, it was impossible to not do a full round of the shop.

For some reason, I'd never thought to go to the baby store before. I didn't know why it hadn't occurred to me—the place was so fun.

I couldn't help picking up toys to show her, wiggling different ones in front of her to catch a reaction. When her eyes widened dramatically at a keyring toy made up of rainbow colors, I kept it in hand. A minute later, when we reached the chew toys and a soft-looking giraffe caught my eye, I grabbed that too.

"Hang on," Ethan said, and I glanced over as he ran back to the front of the store to grab a cart.

When he returned, there was already a blanket set in it, along with another plushie.

I grinned, adding my finds to the collection.

"This is for tummy time, so you can leave her on the floor while she builds her neck and back muscles."

He pointed at the display, and I took a minute before picking one out.

I'd read about tummy time and a million other things. Google had turned into my best friend when I first got Evie, but with so much information, it was hard to know what the most important things to do were. I did put her on her tummy sometimes but in my bed, where I had to be there every moment, watching her just in case.

Suddenly, I realized how good it would be to put her on the floor and know she was fine. I could probably get a cup of coffee without freaking out.

"Found the bath seats!"

Ethan picked one up, putting it into the cart. I couldn't help adding a set of floating toys, and we both grinned. At least Ethan seemed to be enjoying himself. I didn't need to feel too bad about taking too much of his time.

When we reached the beds, it all started to suddenly feel real. Not that having her for the past month wasn't, but I hadn't inserted her into my life properly, had I? She had almost no belongings and no space of her own.

Giving her a bed and blankets and toys... It made it feel like she would belong if I did that.

And that was what I wanted.

If I hadn't been so overwhelmed with keeping her alive, maybe I would have realized that sooner.

"This one is nice," I said, resting my hands on a gray one. It was half the size of the others, perfect for a baby as small as she was, and there was a mobile clipped to the side that hung over the top with plush stars made of shiny fabric. The bedding set was frilly and white, with small stars embroidered on it.

I placed a hand over Evie's back, feeling her warmth through the carrier.

"What do you think?" I asked her, then realized she had fallen asleep again.

"It must be very warm and cozy in there," Ethan said.

I chuckled.

"I guess so. What do you think?" I asked.

"I like it," Ethan said thoughtfully. "But you can use the full-sized cribs for longer."

I glanced at them. There was one just like this in a bigger size, but my apartment was so small... I didn't think it would fit in my bedroom.

"I think I'll have to move soon," I said.

He shook his head.

"No, this one will be great until she's..." He bent forward, reading the sign. "A year and a half. That's perfect. You should get this if it's the one you like."

I nodded. "Okay."

He smiled and waved at one of the employees.

"One of these," he said, indicating the crib.

"With the blanket set," I added, "and the mobile."

Going to pay, I was more excited than I had been in a long time. I couldn't wait to get home and put it all together, to make my home look like somewhere that Evie lived too.

"Aw, who is this sweetheart?" the cashier asked the moment we reached her.

Feeling oddly proud, I unzipped my jacket a bit so she could see her better.

"This is Evie," I said.

"So sweet!" she gushed, scanning our items. "Is she your first?"

I nodded, and the cashier smiled warmly.

"Well, I'm sure she's delighted to have two daddies to dote on her."

I froze for a moment, then glanced at Ethan as my entire face went red hot.

"We're not—I'm not into—"

My voice died, because Ethan was just giving a friendly smile, clearly not interested in arguing.

He caught my eye and shrugged. I looked away.

Did Ethan really not care about being mistaken for a couple? I glanced at him, briefly taking in his classically handsome features. We were so different. Did it really look like we could be together?

For some reason, my heart was racing.

As the cashier finished scanning, I pulled out my wallet, keeping my face carefully blank.

"There's a crib set too," Ethan said.

"I'll get all this part," I said.

He shook his head, handing over his card before I could argue.

The crib and blankets were brought to the front a moment later.

"Oh! One more thing!"

We watched as Ethan rushed through the aisles again. I shrugged at the cashier.

A minute later, he arrived with a car seat in his arms.

"This too."

"But—I don't even drive."

"It's for me," he argued and held it up for her to scan.

I let him do it, but the whole situation felt weird. I had gotten used to being a charity case growing up, but it had been a long time since then. I'd worked full time—granted doing fast food—since I was sixteen. For the last few months, I hadn't been working, but I had plenty of money. More than I ever had before.

The employees helped us take everything outside, and only once we were on the sidewalk and Ethan called for an Uber did the car seat make sense.

"Right," I muttered. "I guess we can't take all of this on the bus."

"Nope," he agreed. "And I wasn't about to send you and Evie on the bus while I took a car."

I shook my head.

"It seems like you think of everything."

Something flickered in his eyes when he looked at me.

"You know, I'm seven years older than you are," he said. "It took me some time to figure it all out. I had to go through my own struggles first."

My heart squeezed.

I hadn't thought of that. In fact, all this time, it had been about me and Evie. Hearing this more human side of Ethan made my stomach hurt. The idea of him going through any sort of darkness bothered me because it didn't fit the image I had of him. I was disappointed to realize I'd put him in a bit of a box: the naturally perfect father figure who would never let anyone down or have any issues of his own.

I swallowed.

"Is that the real reason you're helping me?" I asked.

He smiled sadly.

"Maybe that's part of it. I think that's why I do a lot of the things I do."

He fell silent, his crystal blue gaze fixed on the road.

"Losing my mother and sister when I was a kid was really hard for me. That was why I wanted to start helping children."

Without realizing it, my hand landed on his arm.

"I lost my mom," I said. "When I was six. It's hard for any child... I'm sorry you went through that too... I can't imagine how hard it would have been to lose Liz too."

He looked down at my hand on his arm, then back up, meeting my eyes, something unreadable, visible within.

"What happened to her?" he asked gently.

Even after all these years, I had to force the words out.

"She was hit by a car."

He grimaced.

"I swear it's worse when you don't have any warning. Being able to say goodbye makes it a bit better."

I shrugged.

I couldn't imagine that anything could make it better.

"What about your mom and sister? Was it an accident?"

"It was really unexpected," he started, but before he could say more, a white car with an UBER sticker on the front pulled up in front of us.

CHAPTER 6

ETHAN

NOT THAT I WAS SURPRISED BY HOW SWEET JAIME WAS, BUT the understanding and sympathy in his gaze hit me hard.

I had to *work* to keep it together, to not fall into the memories and pain. After so much time and copious therapy, I didn't often feel like it was a problem.

But after a day spent with Jamie's anxious energy and with Evie being here, I seemed to be falling back into it.

There was nothing wrong with feeling it, I knew that, but I didn't want to on the side of the street, not in front of Jaime... I didn't want to upset him. Not when he kept looking at me like I made the sun rise.

Sitting in the cab, with Evie cradled in her new car seat between us, it hit me that we were almost done. Evie had her bed, her carrier, and plenty of supplies... If I didn't back off soon, Jaime was going to start thinking I was sticking around for other reasons, and yeah... that would have been tempting, if not for his reaction at the store.

I'd been a bit surprised when he'd stopped himself from saying he wasn't into men. The way he looked at me said otherwise, but it could easily just be admiration too. By his age, he would know.

"I'm going to add a stop," I told the driver.

He nodded as I added one on the app, directing us to my house.

My place in Gaynor Heights was close by. As we pulled up to my place, I suddenly felt self-conscious.

First, spending a load of money on a virtual stranger, then bringing him to my house, which made his apartment look even smaller by comparison. I hoped he didn't think I was stuck-up or a showoff.

I wanted Jaime to like me. That much was obvious to me. Just as much as I wanted Evie to be safe and happy, I wanted to get to know Jaime.

One day together and it already felt like our energies matched. I was drawn to him the way I hadn't been to anyone in years.

But he wasn't into me that way, I reminded myself. And that was fine. It wasn't why I was doing this. I'd always felt that if I could make a difference in one child's life, all my years of work would be worth it. This was that child. There would be more, too, but I had chosen Evie and Jaime for obvious reasons. I couldn't allow what had happened twenty-six years ago to happen again.

"I'll just be a second," I said, "Unless you want to come inside while I grab some stuff?"

"I'll stay with Evie," Jaime said.

I nodded and hopped out of the car as soon as it rolled to a stop.

I froze the second I was standing in the parking lot, looking up the steps at the front door. Evan was standing there, waiting for me.

For a moment, his eyes lit up when he saw me. Then, noticing I hadn't moved, Jaime opened his door window.

"What's wrong?" he asked.

From his angle, he couldn't see the front door, but Evan heard his voice and seemed to inflate with anger, crossing his arms.

"Nice," he spat. "Really nice. Set up a date with me and blow me off for someone else without even canceling on me?"

I cringed.

"Ah... shit."

"Yeah," he said, rolling his eyes and marching down the steps.

I expected a slap or something, but Evan just bent down at my open door and glared inside.

"Don't expect him not to blow you off too," he said, then paused, finally noticing Evie.

He grinned and stood, patting me on the shoulder.

"Yeah, that looks like *way* more fun than me."

Chuckling, he walked away, leaving me wanting to bury my head in the ground.

I bent down slowly to look inside.

Both Jaime and Evie were watching me with wide eyes.

"Uh... I'll be right back."

I practically ran inside, straight to my bookshelf, collecting one of each of my books as a gift for them. The whole while, my stomach squirmed. The last thing I wanted was for Jaime to think I was just trying to use him in some sinister way.

I climbed back into the Uber with my tail between my legs, silently cursing myself for forgetting to cancel with Evan.

"Here," I muttered. "For you to read to Evie."

He took them silently, and our gazes lingered, but I had to look away. I knew I should say something about what he had witnessed.

When I chanced a look over, Jaime was still watching me, like he was reading me but was confused. Like I was slightly beyond his comprehension level.

"That guy," I forced out, "we went on a couple of dates. It was fine but I just wasn't interested… I keep trying to blow him off, but he won't take no for an answer. He scheduled himself in with my assistant, and I forgot to cancel."

Being the way he was, Jaime let me finish my awkward speech. I felt awful just saying it. Like I was the biggest dick in the world just because I wasn't interested. And also because now I had to talk about dating other guys with Jaime—not that he was really an option, as I'd already established.

But Jaime shook his head.

"You don't have to explain," he said firmly. "That guy is wrong about you. You're not that type of person."

And with that, he turned to look out the front window again, like the matter was settled.

I sat there, unable to tear my gaze away from Jaime's profile.

CHAPTER 7

JAIME

I COULD FEEL ETHAN'S EYES ON ME, LIKE AN ITCH. I WANTED to look at him, but I forced myself not to, because when I did, I could barely drag my gaze away.

He was gay, or maybe bi. I didn't know. It wasn't my business anyway... although I couldn't help but wonder what the hell he saw in that guy who'd been waiting for him at his doorstep.

Sure, he was kind of a pretty boy, but he seemed a bit wild and kind of prissy too. Ethan Mack, the guy I'd spent the day getting to know, the one who went out of his way to help a stranger, the one who truly cared about children above anything else... he deserved someone different. I wasn't exactly sure who in the world could be good enough for a guy like him, but at the very least, he could do better.

When we got inside, I laid out Evie's tummy-time mat on the living room carpet and set her on it, along with a couple of the toys we got her.

She looked so happy squirming around, reaching for her toys.

"What do you think?" I asked, lying down on the floor in front of her.

She gargled and reached for the giraffe.

I pushed it into her reach, grinning when she managed to grab it and immediately stuffed it into her mouth.

She was drooling happily for a minute and I couldn't take my eyes off of her. It felt good to spend the day doing things for her.

Suddenly, her face started to turn red, her lips dropping into the familiar frown that meant she was about to have a meltdown.

Instinctively, I reached out and rolled her onto her back.

For a moment, she looked stunned by the interruption. Then, just as swiftly, she seemed to remember her giraffe and started to chew on it happily again.

I glanced around, realizing that we had been left alone.

Carefully, I pushed my feet and slowly backed away from Evie.

It felt weird leaving her there alone, but she was fine, I reminded myself.

She was safe, and for once I could walk away without worrying about her.

I found Ethan in my bedroom with all the parts of the crib spread out around him while he read the instructions.

He glanced up and gave me a warm smile.

"Where's Evie?" he asked.

"On her mat," I said. "Do you think it's okay to leave her there?"

"It should be fine for a couple of minutes. Here."

He offered the instructions and I took them, sinking down onto the floor next to him.

Together, the crib didn't seem too complicated. In next

to no time, it was standing. Before we could place down the base though, my paranoia got to me, and I went to check on Evie. To my surprise, she had fallen asleep.

I knelt next to her, watching her breathe for a minute, and then collected myself enough to get her a fresh diaper and change her. Luckily, she didn't wake up while I did, not even when I lifted her carefully into my arms.

Poor, sweet little Evie; she was so vulnerable.

Walking as smoothly as I could, I went back to the bedroom.

Ethan was already securing the arm of the mobile on the side.

He glanced over and raised his eyebrows.

"Just a second," he said, quickly pulling out the bed set and arranging it. Then, he set one of the thin baby blankets on top that Liz had left for her daughter.

When it was all done, he motioned for me to come closer.

Getting the idea, I very carefully laid Evie down on the blanket and wrapped her up as best I could. I was still getting the hang of the burrito thing, but this was the one time that, when it was done, I didn't berate myself for how it looked.

She was in a crib, wrapped up nice and warm, and she was fast asleep. What more could I ask for?

I shook my head in wonder.

"This will make a big difference," I said quietly. "It's like she really belongs here now."

A hand landed on my shoulder, squeezing gently.

"Come on," Ethan said, gesturing to the door.

I followed him back to the living room.

"Look, it's late, neither of us had any dinner either," he chuckled, "so I'll get out of your hair and let you wind down and hopefully have a proper sleep in your bed for once."

My heart squeezed at his words. I wanted to ask him if that was it. Would I ever see him again?

"Right. Sure," I said.

He gave me a smile, but it was strained at the edges.

I swallowed.

"Listen, thank you for everything. You didn't need to do any of that."

"I know I didn't," he said. "It sounded like you had the money to buy all that stuff. I still wanted to do it for you though."

Why? I wanted to ask. He couldn't be *that* selfless. No one was.

"We got a pretty big insurance payout when my dad died last year," I found myself saying instead.

He stared at me for a long moment.

"Sounds like it's been a rough while for you," he said. "But it'll get better."

The confidence with which he said that seemed to uncoil something inside me.

"You really think so?" I asked. "I'm not really sure what to do with the money. I wanted to go to college, but I'll need my GED first. And of course, now that I have Evie, I know I should drive, but—anyway, none of that matters."

I cut myself short, feeling like an idiot. Ethan had already helped me enough. He didn't need any more sob stories from me. That was a terrible way to try to make someone stick around for a bit longer. And that was what I was doing. I didn't want him to leave.

I wasn't that hungry, but I'd happily make us dinner

and watch movies with him and, basically, do anything to make him stick around.

"Sometimes we need people to hold our hands through things. There's nothing wrong with that."

I managed to nod at his words.

"You can always call me if you need help with anything," he said kindly. "You have my number."

I forced another nod.

Shit. This was it. This weird, dreamlike day was ending, and I wasn't ready for that. I wanted—I didn't know what I wanted, except for Ethan to not leave.

I couldn't pull my gaze away, his eyes were so penetrating that I felt weak.

Finally, he took a breath, readying himself to go. He started to turn toward the door.

Without realizing what I was going to do, my hand landed on his arm. As soon as he started to turn back toward me, my mouth was on his.

I pulled back almost at once, but his lips seared mine like a brand.

My hand flew up, touching them in shock.

"I—I'm so sorry. I don't know why I did that. I panicked."

My heart was racing a mile a minute, but Ethan looked calm.

Of course he was. He was used to kissing guys. He was probably used to guys throwing themselves at him too. Hell, who wouldn't? He was the epitome of a dream man. He was good-looking enough to be a movie star but chose to write kids' books. He could spend his time and money on anything, but instead, he chose to spend them on me and Evie and—*shit*, I was going to kiss him again.

I pressed forward, my hands went into his short hair,

and this time when our lips met, I didn't immediately jump in the opposite direction.

I leaned in closer, moaning when he finally started to kiss me back. His strong hands wove into my hair, holding me steady while his soft lips moved hungrily against mine.

Ethan felt overwhelming and *overpowering*. The way he moved forced me to follow. His lips parted, mine parted. His tongue slipped into my mouth, mine met it. He bit my lip, surprisingly hard, and I gasped. Then those strong hands I wanted to lean into, pushed me back.

I didn't get it. At first, I thought that he was going to steer me somewhere good, like onto the couch, but then I saw the regretful look in his eyes and felt my entire being close down around me.

"Stop," he said unnecessarily. "You don't have to do this."

My lips were still tingling, my heart racing, my cock, clearly not aware that Ethan had put the brakes on, was pressing the front of my jeans eagerly.

"What?" I asked.

"You don't owe me anything," Ethan said in frustration. "I *wanted* to help out today. Not because I thought I would get something out of it."

Suddenly I felt dirty.

"That's not…"

"Then what?" he demanded.

I hadn't imagined Ethan could work up a temper. It looked all wrong on his face.

I was shaking my head, mind racing, unable to think up an argument.

Being him though, he waited, still breathing hard as his frustration faded to—*guilt*.

"I—I didn't mean to make you feel that way," I finally said.

His brows dipped in confusion.

"Jaime, at the shop, you said that you weren't into... well, that was all you said, actually, but I assumed you were going to say *men*."

I stared at him as I remembered that little fact.

"Right. Yeah," I muttered. "I guess I'm not as straight as I thought."

That was an interesting realization to make *after* making out with a guy.

"Great," I groaned. "Another thing to add to the list of things to panic about."

I tried to laugh it off, but it came out bitter and trembling.

Unable to face Ethan, I moved around him to the couch, collapsing onto it while my heart raced.

Thankfully, my forming boner had taken a hint and was retreating back into the warmth of my boxers, so I didn't have to worry about that part at least.

"So you kissed me because you actually *want* me?"

"Yeah. I guess I'm bi," I said, my mind still reeling.

"It might not be that..." Ethan said gently.

I looked up at him, biting my lip nervously.

"What else would it be?" I asked, laughing awkwardly. I knew I was probably bright red on top of everything.

"You've been so stressed, Jaime," he said, moving toward me.

"You probably just need to unwind... and I'm here."

He slid down onto his knees in front of me, and my entire body flushed with heat when I saw the look in his eyes.

Penetrating as usual and filled with heat.

His hand slid onto my knee, resting there for a moment while he spoke.

"You need to relax and have a good night's sleep. You've had so much on your plate. You need someone to take care of you for a change."

His hand slid up my inseam, so damn confident, just like with everything he did. My breath caught in my throat.

"Will you let me take care of you?"

I nodded breathlessly, even though I had no idea how to go forward with this. But I'd instigated the whole thing and I wanted it. I wanted to get off and I wanted it to be Ethan getting me there. That was all I knew. I couldn't even remember the last time I'd jacked off since having Evie to constantly watch made it harder to be alone. Yet when Ethan's hands moved up, over my forming erection, and I saw the way he was looking at me, I nearly ran again.

It took effort to force myself to remain still. My hands were shaking so hard that it felt like they were vibrating.

Ethan's warm hand retreated, sliding back to my knee. His other one landed over my hand, squeezing gently.

"Why don't you shut your eyes, and try to relax," he suggested. "I'll take care of everything."

Before I could answer, he leaned over my lap, pressing his lips to mine again and, fuck, he was such a good kisser. Even the scrape of his stubble felt good.

This time, when his hand slipped over my zipper again and rested there, I twitched toward it and my breath caught in my throat.

"Let me take care of everything," he whispered again, this time against my lips.

I moaned and nodded.

If there was anyone I could trust to make me feel good and take all my troubles away, it was Ethan. The fact that it was him was comforting and as soon as I agreed, every bit of defense and resistance I had, melted out of me.

I gave myself over completely. Hopefully, he knew I would follow his every word, wherever it would lead me.

CHAPTER 8

ETHAN

I knew I shouldn't be doing what I was doing.

Jaime was vulnerable and desperate for support, and I was a celebrity to him. He looked up to me and admired me; that much had been clear from the get-go.

Yet here I was, pushing his shoulders back until he got the idea and let his head fall onto the back of the couch, his eyes swooping shut.

He was even sexier than I'd let myself think. The line of his jaw, his neck, the warm, solid tone of his skin. I bent forward, nipping his Adam's apple and relishing the way he gasped. When I took his hands and spread them out over the back of the sofa, he didn't even try to move them. In fact he went with every movement, like a doll, letting me position him just how I wanted.

I regretted that I'd left his t-shirt on, but I didn't want to stop now when he was so *pliable*.

My stomach dropped.

When he'd first kissed me, I'd wanted it at the same time that I had been annoyed by it. The second that I'd realized he really wanted me though… I swallowed.

I wouldn't take advantage—okay, maybe it was too late for that, but I wasn't about to back away now. I couldn't walk away.

But I also wouldn't push it. I would do what I'd said and get him off. The thought made me groan in anticipation, and his cock, still trapped in his clothes, moved in response.

Unable to stop myself, I gripped the waistband of his jeans and dropped down over the mound, parting my lips softly on top, not applying enough pressure to really give him anything as I exhaled, warming him.

His entire body shuddered, but I kept going, heating his cock until a whine tore from his throat and his hips jerked up, desperate for more.

I held him down a moment longer, being even more of a bastard by giving him *something*, just not what he wanted by gently dragging my teeth over the fabric there. He stilled, but when I glanced up, his chest was rising and falling hard and fast.

Swallowing, I pulled back, taking Jaime's jeans down with me. He lifted his hips to help but didn't otherwise move. His eyes were squeezed shut and his fists were clenched. I almost wanted to apologize for teasing him, but instead, I couldn't help taking a moment just to look at him. Seeing him spread out in front of me like a gift that I got to play with made me feel *powerful*.

His knees were splayed, his cock hard and decently big. More than a mouthful, I thought, and my mouth watered in anticipation.

The moment my lips touched his cock, it twitched and precome spurted from the tip. Unable to resist, I took it into my mouth. We both moaned as I sucked it clean.

I had to force myself off when more suddenly splashed into my mouth.

Jaime was trembling, making soft, almost distressed sounds every time he exhaled. He was so fucking cute and sexy at the same time. How was it that I still felt an overwhelming desire to protect him even while I was fucking him?

"You're so sexy," I whispered, trailing my fingers over his thighs, his hips, up his waist—anywhere but his cock. I wanted to drag this out.

"Yeah?" he gasped.

"Mmhm."

I tweaked his nipples, then did it again when he twitched and gasped.

It was easy to take this slow. I was already dreading it ending, dreading walking to my car with a raging, untouched hard-on. But this wasn't about me. Later, when Jaime came down from this sleepless, stressed haze that he lived in, I hoped he wouldn't feel like I'd taken advantage of him. I was the older gay man who spent the day buying him things. but all I could do was trust that he had meant what he said about being attracted to me.

"Please," he suddenly whispered, twisting his hips back toward my mouth.

"Not yet," I whispered, but slid a hand around the base, squeezing while I pressed a hot kiss to the frenulum.

He cried out, finally collapsing from his position, spread out on the couch, curling in toward me instead, his hands clasping the back of my neck with sudden strength.

"Please," he groaned into my hair. "Keep sucking me."

Before I gave in to his desperate request, I slid a finger into my mouth, getting it wet.

When I took his cock deep into my mouth, I pressed it against his small hole.

He gasped, stilling as it slid into him.

Pulling off, I released his cock, pressing him back with a firm hand in the center of his chest.

He fell back against the couch, watching me with blown-out eyes, his lips parted.

"Has anyone ever done this to you before?" I asked breathlessly, thrusting my digit deep into him. His hips lifted a bit and gasped softly, shaking his head.

A pleased rumble ran through my chest as I slowly finger-fucked him, eager to make the first time someone was inside him enough to make him crave it over and over again. The way his hole clung to me, so tight even just on my finger, made my cock ache with envy.

Groaning, I bent down over him, taking his length into my mouth, bobbing in rhythm to my finger in his ass.

When I crooked it at the right angle, hitting his prostate, his entire body shuddered.

A couple more thrusts and he was writhing and crying out, his muscles clenching around me while his hips bucked into my mouth.

I was ready for the first spurt of hot liquid in the back of my throat and swallowed it down, moaning in pleasure, precome seeping from my tip.

He held still there for a moment, letting me milk the last drops from him, then released the breath he'd been holding and collapsed back into the couch cushions, his length slipping out from between my lips.

I swallowed, trying to collect myself before I met Jaime's gaze.

His dark eyes were sleepy and sated with none of the fear and worry he'd had in them since I met him. He looked better than ever that way, relaxed and mussed up, his silky brown hair a fluffy tangle, his cheeks and lips red.

Unable to help myself, I practically dove in for a kiss, capturing his mouth against mine, my arms wrapping around him, tongue delving into his mouth tasting him again. *One last time*, I thought, and sadness hit me.

Jaime didn't notice, threading his fingers into my hair and sighing against my kiss as it turned languid.

"That was good," he whispered against my lips.

"Yeah, baby," I agreed, subconsciously stroking his naked thighs and pelvis.

He let out a long breath, his arms falling around my shoulders.

"Fuck," he moaned quietly, "you're going to get me hard again."

I stilled, realizing what I was doing.

"I could keep you up all night," I murmured, sighing, "but that's the opposite of what I was trying to do."

I forced myself to pull back. He let me go, but only, I suspected, because he was already half asleep.

"Get to bed," I said. "Quickly, before Evie wakes up for her next feed."

He blinked at me sleepily.

"What about you?" he asked.

For a moment, I thought he meant for me to come to sleep with him and *yes* was on the tip of my tongue. Then his gaze flickered down to the front of my pants. I was rock hard and aching, desperate for his touch.

"I'm fine," I managed to say to save face. "I'm going to head home."

Disappointment flickered in his gaze before he tore it away and bent down, grabbing the boxers still around his ankles.

I had to get up to make room for him. My knees screamed after spending so much time on the floor. Carpet or not, it was cement under there and I wasn't quite as young as I used to be, although I hadn't noticed they'd gone numb until that moment.

Jaime stood, pulling his boxers up and kicking his jeans free.

Standing now, face to face, back at square one, almost like the last half-hour hadn't happened at all, was surreal.

"Thanks," Jaime said, touching my arm, "for everything today… it made everything feel better. Like I wasn't so alone."

My heart warmed all the way through.

"That means the world to me," I said and I meant it.

CHAPTER 9

JAIME

EVIE WOKE UP TWICE DURING THE NIGHT, ONCE FOR A FEED and the second time for a diaper change.

I was surprised by how well she was taking to being in a crib but chose not to question it when it meant I actually got to sleep in my bed for once.

I'd forgotten what it was like to stretch out and have my head on a pillow. *Heaven*. Of course, it helped that I was extra relaxed after a bit of help from my guardian angel.

A small smile lifted my lips and I buried my face in my pillow, remembering. I was already half hard from sleep and thinking about Ethan, the sensual way that he touched me and took control, but didn't force it, made a shiver travel through my body.

It was interesting how different a man could feel and touch and act. I hadn't thought much about being with a man before, but being with Ethan last night had made me think it would be easy. Not just in bed, but in everything.

Evie let out a loud cry, cutting my line of thought short.

"Okay baby, you come first," I told her, climbing

quickly out of bed and going to her crib. Her eyes were squeezed shut, face twisted into a cranky expression.

"Oh, hello Evie. How did you sleep? You sick of being bundled up like that?"

She let out a loud wail, but instead of setting me on edge, the sound made me chuckle.

"Okay, okay, one second."

I quickly unwrapped her, melting at how she stretched her limbs the moment she was free.

I lifted her up, patting her back while I carried her into the kitchen to grab a bottle.

She quieted down as soon as it was in her mouth, sucking the nipple greedily.

When she was done, I laid her down on her mat and went to make breakfast.

Everything felt *lighter* all of a sudden. From one day to the next, everything had changed. I didn't have to balance my girl in one arm while I made toast. There was time for real food this morning and since we'd skipped dinner last night, I was starving.

I went all out, scrambled eggs and fried bacon, made oatmeal and toast, and carried it all out to the table where I could sit and watch Evie playing.

She loved her new toys and was shaking one of them, staring up at the ceiling. As I ate, she started to make happy babbling sounds, like she was conversing with someone. Her small voice was so cute that after a while, I just rested my chin on my palm and watched her, smiling.

Eventually, unable to help myself, I pulled out my phone and recorded her.

I tapped my hands on the table a few times before deciding to forward the video to my most recent contact.

I didn't know if Ethan wanted to keep talking to me. I

may have been his charity case for the month for all I knew. Maybe he took lots of boys around, shopped for them, then ended the night sucking them off.

I bit my lip, knowing that wasn't true and shaking the intrusive thought away.

Before I could back out, I hit send on the video and added a message.

> Good call on the tummy time mat and toys. She loves them.

I stared at my phone, waiting for a response. Ethan didn't disappoint, sending one almost straight away.

> That's insanely cute.

> What are you up to today?

My heart raced as his second message came through. I looked around, realizing for the first time that I didn't make plans anymore. I didn't do much of anything. I just stayed home and cared for Evie. But the sun was shining through the windows. It was a beautiful day and Evie deserved to see it.

> I'm going to take Evie for a walk. What about you?

> I'll be doing some work today. Writing, editing, marketing. Part of the author grind.

> Sounds fun.

All but the marketing, yeah. I hate using social media, but kind of have to.

Well, I'll keep an eye out for your posts.

Please don't. They're so cringy. I might just put up a clip from one of the recent episodes.

I grinned. It was weird to see behind the veil. This man who I considered a local celebrity spoke about his TV show and books as though they were regular jobs.

Evie's babbling suddenly got louder, drawing my attention as she kicked. It looked like she was moments from enjoyment turning into crying, so I set my phone down and went down onto the floor with her.

"Ah, I see why you like it down here," I said to her.

She watched me with those wide blue eyes. I assumed she'd gotten them from her father, because Liz's eyes were brown, like mine and both of our parents.

"We've been cooped up for far too long," I said. "Come on, let's go for a walk."

Getting her dressed, I realized I probably needed to take her clothes shopping soon. Her belongings were starting to get small already. Her little feet pressed a bit too tightly into her onesie and the sleeves were just above the wrist.

It hadn't felt like I'd had her long enough for her to grow this much. I paused, realizing that this was the very pastel purple outfit that Liz had delivered her to me in. For the first time it hit me that amidst a severe addiction and panic over caring for a newborn, she'd still bought Evie a collection of adorable clothes.

For the first time since she had abandoned her

daughter with me, my heart ached for Liz. Sure, I'd felt regret for her and the life she'd lived so far, but it hadn't really hit me until this moment just how hard this must have been for her.

Tears stung my eyes. Taking a shuddering breath, I pulled Evie close, hugging her to my chest and inhaling her soft, baby scent.

"I'll take care of you," I promised. "From now on, everything is going to be smooth sailing for us."

And for Liz too, I hoped. I didn't know what the future held for her, but I wanted that to be a happy, healthy life. One that meant we could be close again and somehow move on from all the stuff we'd been through together.

Swallowing down the lump in my throat, I took my time fastening Evie into her carrier.

I zipped her into my jacket, and it was so nice and warm and cozy, even for me, having her right against my heart and comfortable.

When I picked up my phone to stick it into my pocket, there was another message from Ethan.

> It was nice getting to know you both yesterday.

I smiled, my heart squeezing.

Ethan was so damn sweet and polite. I'd never known anyone who spoke the way that he did. Clear and calm and honest...

Maybe there were other people like him out there. I wouldn't know. Life had been too much to handle. For my whole family. For a while, I'd been like Liz, chasing highs and then crashing low. The friends I'd made liked to party too and in a group, it was easier to try to bury yourself.

The partying had been too much for me though and I'd managed to drag myself out of it, but Liz had already been in too deep. She was older and had been doing it longer. Maybe that was why.

I shoved my phone into my pocket, mood fluctuating from the contentedness I'd woken to this morning.

Walking out into the sunshine helped though.

And I'd forgotten that there was a park nearby.

I sat down on the bench, watching the kids play while parents watched like hawks. One mom's eyes widened dramatically when her toddler tried to walk down the bars. She made it to her child just in time to offer a helping hand. It made me smile seeing that I wasn't the only paranoid one.

For the first time, I thought, maybe I wasn't terrible at this. Maybe the way I'd been feeling was normal.

And in the summer, when Evie was a bit older, I could walk down with her, put her in the baby swing, or even go down the slide with her in my lap.

I wasn't used to the tingling hope building in my chest, and I knew just who to blame for it.

CHAPTER 10

ETHAN

You know, you really changed my outlook on things.

In a good way?

Yeah.

...

I feel like I can do this now. Like I just have to take things one step at a time. But actually, I'm excited. There's a bunch of stuff I've been wanting for a long time but I didn't do anything about any of it. Now, I want to start planning things.

Yeah? That's great to hear Jaime. Genuinely have me smiling ear to ear.

What are you going to do first?

Not sure.

> Find a babysitter so I can have some time to decide? Lol

> Well, let me know as soon as you find one.

> Why?

> So I can take you for dinner.

I STARED AT MY PHONE FOR FAR TOO LONG, CHEWING MY LIP while I waited anxiously for an answer.

Trust me at thirty to fall for the straight guy, but I couldn't get him, or the feeling of his hard cock, out of my mind. I'd woken up this morning, achingly hard with his fantom length buried down my throat, remembering so vividly that it felt like it was happening again.

He'd let me do it once. What was to stop it from happening again? And then over and over after that?

There was just something about Jaime. Maybe it was the way his deep vulnerability showed on the surface. Maybe it was the way that he looked at me. Maybe it was fate. Hell, all I knew was that I wanted to hold him again and kiss him mercilessly and spoil him and his sweet little girl rotten.

"*Wow.* Someone's got it bad."

I looked up, realizing that Naomi was leaning against the makeup desk watching me with her arms crossed, a playful smile on her face that only grew when I promptly turned red and tucked my phone hastily into my pocket.

Her jaw dropped.

"No way! I was just joking. Did you actually meet someone that you like?"

I rolled my eyes, but my cheeks were getting hotter by the minute and she gasped.

"It's not that. It was a work message."

"Uh-huh," she said skeptically.

Thankfully, Arty, my producer interrupted by walking in, a big grin on his bearded face.

"Hey buddy," he said, slapping me on the shoulder, "our ratings are up again!"

"No way."

"Yeah man, people love their McIntosh apples."

He winked, and I shook my head in wonder.

Getting to do this show had been a bit of a shot in the dark to begin with. The fact that so many people were tuning in now, in Gaynor and the surrounding towns, was awe-inspiring.

"Ready to get another one in the can?" he asked.

I nodded.

"I sure am."

I stood up, unable to help checking my phone one more time. Jaime still hadn't responded.

Disappointed, I pulled open the top drawer and tucked it inside with my wallet before turning to go to the stage.

"Aren't you forgetting your guitar?" Naomi asked, watching with that amused smile still plastered on her face.

"Shit," I muttered. "And I forgot to tune it."

I picked it up, slinging the strap over my shoulder with a sigh. Hopefully, no one was in a rush today. My head clearly wasn't quite in it yet.

"Oh, you are so not getting away without telling me the details," Naomi swore.

"Fine," I chuckled. "After the show."

She grinned triumphantly.

————

IT TOOK EFFORT, BUT I WAS ABLE TO PUSH JAIME FROM MY mind while I worked. Focusing on the script and the story I told today—a classic, The Tortoise and the Hare—took over. I'd worked hard on that skill over the years, of focusing on the moment and being present. That didn't mean that the second we were done filming I didn't immediately remember our unfinished conversation.

Since it was such a small production, there was very little staff. Greg, the all-arounder, took care of the lights and camera, while Arty, the producer took care of the basics, like renting the studio and working with the hired editing company. Aside from that, it was me and Naomi. There was no makeup crew or anything fancy like that, and, today, I was grateful for the lack of personnel, because that meant as soon as I thanked the guys for their work, I was free to take off to the makeup table to check my phone.

"Holy hell, who has you wrapped around their little finger?" Naomi demanded playfully. "You promised gossip!"

There was a new message from Jaime. My heart leaped.

I would love to see you again ASAP. If you know where to find a babysitter, please let me know. lol

"Don't tell me it's Evan?" she demanded, gasping dramatically. "Oh my god, did he finally win you over when he dropped by? You spend the weekend together?"

I looked at her, not even following.

"Huh?"

She stared at me.

"Okay, not Evan, then."

"Evan?" I blinked. "What? Hell no. That guy is too wild for me. He showed up and made a bit of a scene, actually."

Her brows shot up.

"No way. What happened?"

I bit my lip, suddenly remembering her dismissal of Jaime at the reading when I'd first met him. I couldn't hide things from her though and knew that.

"Remember that guy from the reading?" I asked tentatively.

She frowned.

"You don't mean leather jacket guy, do you?"

I shrugged.

"He's really sweet," I argued.

"Ethan," she said slowly, "that guy was low-key stalkerish."

"No. He wasn't. He's a good person. He's just been down on his luck and—"

"And wanted to come meet a kids show host?"

I shrugged self-consciously.

"Yeah, well, he was right to come to me. He needed help."

Her frown deepened.

"Then he should go to some sort of therapy. Don't tell me you actually went and helped this stranger—"

"Stop."

I'd never been angry at Naomi. We'd met about three years ago when I first felt the need for an assistant to help me arrange my schedule and daily life. Between book marketing, appearance schedules, and literally anything else I could need from an assistant, she'd been a godsend. Of course, part of that was because we were always on the same page and had been fast friends from the get-go. It felt immediately *wrong* to feel like she was being an asshole, because I knew she always spoke from the heart—which only left one explanation... that I wasn't thinking straight. I didn't like that train of thought. When it came to Jaime, there was more to it than that.

I took a deep breath, processing before continuing.

"He didn't ask me for anything," I said. "I just insisted because—"

"Because you think he's cute?" she challenged.

"Yeah," I admitted. "I'm not going to lie. I'm really attracted to him. That's not why though."

I paused, wondering how much to say.

"He has a little baby girl and he had no idea what to do with her. He was really overwhelmed and scared and... he has no one to turn to, at all."

Naomi watched me closely, her wide eyes unreadable.

"He didn't ask me for anything," I repeated.

After a long moment, her gaze softened.

"And you really like him?"

I nodded.

"Doesn't mean it's going to go anywhere," I said.

"But you want it to?"

I didn't answer because I didn't know how.

No matter what Jaime let me do to him the other day, it didn't mean he suddenly wanted to get with a guy in a deeper way. Even if he "wasn't as straight as he thought he was." If he went for it though, for the first time I could remember, I wanted to jump feet first into a relationship. For some reason, I was entranced. I wanted to get to know everything about him.

"And does he know why you're so eager to help?" she asked gently, her gaze filled with compassion.

Trust Naomi to read through me just like that.

I shook my head, unable to meet her gaze.

With a heavy sigh, Naomi reached out, placing a warm hand on my arm.

"Well, you might want to tell him before you get in any deeper. You might also want to get to know him a bit better before committing. Just saying. I mean, he did find you from TV."

"The book signings are public," I argued.

"Don't think he was there for the books," she said, making me blush.

"Well, we aren't going to be spending much time together at all unless we find a babysitter," I said, giving her a look.

She groaned dramatically.

"When and where?"

CHAPTER 11
JAIME

I stood outside the Lupo Ristorante and Bar, trying not to fidget under the streetlights while I waited for Ethan. The caption below the menu in the window said *sophisticated Italian fare and wines*. There was no way I could go in there. Like an idiot, I hadn't looked the place up before leaving the house. I wasn't dressed well enough to enter. Hell, as far as I knew, there was a dress code and I would be turned away at the door.

And I'd thought I looked nice in clean black jeans and a dark green, long-sleeved shirt. If I had a different jacket, or shoes, maybe it would have been okay, but my beat-up Nike runners and leather jacket didn't really elevate the look.

"Jaime, what the hell!"

I turned, shock reverberating through my body at a familiar voice.

"Mark!" I said, as my old friend walked up the side-walk toward me, arms out for a friendly hug.

I returned it, still in shock when he patted my back. When he pulled back I noticed the slightly vacant look in his blue eyes. It was only seven, but starting early had been the norm before. Looked like it still was. I shuddered at the thought of having a hangover at six in the morning when Evie would wake me up.

"Where have you been, man?" he demanded, grinning. "I called a couple times."

He *had* but that was months ago. Once I'd said I didn't want to drink or do anything harder a couple times in a row, those calls had dried up.

I forced a shrug.

"I don't know, I've just been holed up with the baby, you know?"

"Right..."

He nodded as though just remembering and chuckled.

"Can't imagine it, gotta be honest."

I chuckled awkwardly.

"Yeah, it's crazy."

"So, what are you doing out here?" he asked. "I'm heading downtown to meet Craig and Dave and the gang. Come with."

"I can't," I said at once. "I'm meeting someone."

"Yeah? Who? They can come too."

Just then, Ethan suddenly caught my attention, walking up to us with a smile and flushed cheeks from hurrying. His long, black jacket was open, hands tucked in the pockets. He grinned when our eyes met, and my body flooded with heat.

"Hey, sorry. Hope you weren't waiting long," he said as he reached me. He didn't kiss me, but I got the impression he would have if I'd been standing here alone, and I was hit with disappointment. For two days leading up to this date, I'd been on edge wondering how Ethan would be with me, or how I *wanted* him to be with me. Now I knew. I wanted his lips and hands and eyes on me.

I bit my lip.

"I just got here," I said, swallowing under his sharp gaze.

"Alright, I'll leave you two to it," Mark suddenly said, reminding me that he was still there. He smirked and then walked away, snickering. I watched him go, my heart hammering.

Was this what it felt like to get outed accidentally?

Considering I'd only had a few days to even come around to the fact that I wanted a man, I wasn't sure how to feel about it.

Ethan's hand landed on my back.

"You okay?" he asked, and I found myself leaning into his comforting touch, forgetting everything else.

"Yeah," I said, "I am."

Except for the fact that I'd missed out on that kiss I wanted.

If I had any bit of courage, I would have leaned in and kissed him myself. But my feet were fused to the ground, and I couldn't bring myself to do anything other than stare at him.

His hand slid up, then down my spine and I nearly purred.

"Come on," he said, and his hand slipped down to my wrist, holding it.

The confident way he led me toward the door eased any concern I had. The fact that Ethan always knew what he was doing was comforting. Just like the other night, it felt relaxing to let him take the lead.

Inside Lupo Ristorante, the lights were dim and

artfully aimed at the bricks on the wall and the glass tabletops.

It was a beautiful space, but I didn't take much notice of it all. Ethan held my attention.

As we were led to our table where a candle had been lit and dishes and cutlery already placed, Ethan finally released me. I sat across from him, not paying any attention as the server listed the wines and specials.

Ethan must have sensed my desire to leave it all to him, because he ordered us a bottle, and appetizer, his gaze drawn to mine every couple of seconds.

"You look amazing," he said, leaning across the table the moment the waiter walked away.

Relief and warmth swept through me.

"Thanks," I muttered, and Ethan reached across the table.

Without thinking, I took his hand, shivering as he stroked a thumb over my knuckles, gazing into my eyes.

"I'm glad you agreed to come to dinner," he said. "I was worried I wouldn't see you again."

"I was worried about that too," I admitted.

Apparently, that was the right thing to say, because his smile made my insides flutter with excitement.

"How is Evie?" he asked.

"Good. I may be imagining it, but she seems happier than before. She fusses less. Still isn't used to being left in the crib, but she'll come around I'm sure."

"She will," Ethan agreed. "And what about you? Are you starting to adjust? Figuring things out?"

"Uh, yeah kind of," I said with an awkward chuckle. "I mean, I wrote a list, but don't know how to do anything on it yet."

Ethan's brows shot up.

"Why? What's on the list?"

Using my free hand, I reached into my pocket for my phone, pulling up my notes at the same moment that the waiter arrived with the wine.

I waited while Ethan ordered two of the specials. I nodded at his look.

"That would be great," I said, not that I remembered what the specials were.

"Let me see that list," Ethan said the moment he was gone.

I handed him my phone, taking a nervous sip of the wine while he skimmed it.

"So, *learn how to drive. Set up appointment for driver's test*," he read.

I nodded.

"I got my learner's a while ago, but it's about to expire."

"*Get GED. Research colleges*," he went on. "*Decide field of study and apply. Shop for clothes for Evie. Find part-time job. Find babysitter/childcare.*"

He handed me back my phone, looking thoughtful.

"This is good, Jaime," he said. "They're good steps to take, especially when you have a child to care for. I don't know how much your father left you but it's good to be self-sufficient."

"Exactly!" I enthused. "It's the stuff I wanted to do before I got Evie. I stopped thinking about it for a while, but now, suddenly, I want it even more."

"Having kids does that, from what I hear. It pushes people in the best way."

I smiled.

"Of course, I can't really do any of it without the

bottom one. This is my first time out without her. It feels weird."

He chuckled.

"I bet."

"Thanks for getting your friend to come watch her. Naomi was really nice."

"Yeah?" he asked. "She is great."

Something about the way Ethan said it made my gaze narrow. He sounded kind of surprised.

"What is it? Do you not actually like her?"

His eyes widened.

"What? No, she's probably my best friend. She's fantastic. And good with kids. She has a nephew who is about four now who she babysits all the time," he added, "so I'm sure she'll be great with Evie."

I stared at him for a long time.

"So, it's not that *you* don't like her, you're surprised that *I* do."

He sighed.

"It's not that," he grudgingly admitted. "She's protective of me, that's all... I guess I had been kind of worried she would grill you or something like that. When I told her about you, she was worried."

For a minute, I was genuinely confused. How would I be any sort of threat to Ethan? Sure, I wasn't exactly a small guy, but Ethan had a few inches on me, and he looked strong. But that wasn't the only reason someone would be worried about who their friend was dating.

"She thinks I'm using you."

Just saying it made me feel dirty suddenly. Ethan's grimace didn't help. I sat up straighter, pulling my hand back as the bubble of intimacy between us popped.

"Hey," Ethan said, leaning across the table before I could spiral, "what does she know?"

"I showed up at your reading and the next thing, you're buying me things and… and…"

I couldn't add the last part about us getting intimate because suddenly the wonderful day we'd spent together felt tarnished.

"Remember how I insisted? How I showed up at your place and invited myself in?"

I looked up, meeting Ethan's sincere gaze.

"You didn't make me do buy you anything. Even when we got to the till, you tried to pay."

"Right," I agreed, but now that we were talking about it, and now that I had *thought* about it… "Was that why? So *you* could get something from *me*?"

My voice came out small and uncertain and the moment it was out of my lips, and I saw his expression, I realized how stupid I was to have said it.

"Is that how you feel?" Ethan asked. "Because if so, if you came onto me because you felt pressured or like you owed me—"

"No. It was the opposite."

I swallowed and physically shook myself.

"Shit. I'm sorry. I know you're not like that. It was just an intrusive thought for a second."

My heart was pounding with guilt as I sat under his scrutinizing gaze.

"The reason I came onto you was because—"

He waited while I forced the words out.

"It was because I like the way you look at me. I like the way you talk and the nice things you say. That day it felt like I got to know you. I thought I wouldn't see you again and I wanted to make the most of it."

His cheeks darkened while I spoke.

Under the table, his feet found mine. He pressed our ankles together.

"Thank you for being so open with me," he whispered. "Now I guess it should be my turn... I'm not as innocent as I'm making out."

I stilled.

"Jaime, I'm deeply attracted to you. I was from the moment I laid eyes on you. It's not why I helped you, but I would be lying if I pretended it wasn't something I was aware of as soon as I saw you."

He swallowed, his gaze dropping to his wine glass.

"That was why I didn't want you to touch me or get me off," he admitted. "I didn't want it to feel like that was my reason for being there. It really wasn't."

Well, how the hell was I supposed to be mad at that?

If he hadn't vocalized how much he liked sucking me and fingering me, and kissing me with hot moans, I probably would have wondered, but knowing he was as into me as I was into him was a turn on.

My stomach swooped, cock thickening in my jeans.

"So, what do you think?" Ethan asked, nudging my foot playfully. The slight smirk on his lips shot straight to my cock.

"About the wine?" I asked. "I can't tell the difference between wines to be honest. I hope it wasn't too expensive."

Ethan burst into laughter just as the servers arrived with our meals.

It turned out to be a chicken alfredo. I couldn't complain. The food was amazing, the company even better, but I still wanted to get the hell out of there as fast as possible.

"How's the food?" Ethan asked.

"Amazing," I said, voicing my thoughts. "But I still think we should skip dessert."

He pinned me with his gaze, like a butterfly on a cushion, I thought, powerless to fight his desires. Luckily, judging by the heat in them, they were in line with mine.

Suddenly, he set his fork down.

"I'm done," he said. "You?"

I had to glance down at my plate to check. I could barely remember. Nope. There was half of it still there, and on Ethan's too, and half a bottle of wine.

"All done," I agreed.

CHAPTER 12

ETHAN

THERE WAS SOMETHING ABOUT JAIME THAT TOOK ME OVER completely. The shape of his lips, his beautiful doe eyes hot with desire, the way he carried himself and opened up, the timbre of his voice—okay, his incredible round ass and narrow hips too—knowing what was in his jeans and how it felt filling my mouth.

I had to wave the waiter over for the bill because my cock was rock hard, and I didn't want to get up and go to the front to pay. I had to spend a couple of minutes insisting that the food was fantastic but we were going to be late for a movie if we didn't run. The good tip reassured him. All the while, Jaime was watching me. Sometimes I'd catch him watching my neck or my lips or my hands, biting his lips and nearly making me forget pretenses and just drag him out of there without paying at all.

Finally, the waiter walked away and I stood at once.

This time, Jaime's eyes dropped to my cock, bulging the front of my pants.

He took a shaky breath, his gaze heavy with desire.

"Come on," I growled.

That was accidental, the way my voice dropped to a deep rumble, but Jaime's eyes shot to mine in surprise and he stood at once.

I was gratified to see that he was hard too. My mouth watered at the sight and I hooked an arm around his waist, leading him out into the chilly night air.

"Shit," I muttered, pulling him closer, "wish I'd found a closer spot."

My car was around the corner, but Jaime didn't seem to mind, leaning against my side as we walked.

The moment he was in the passenger seat and the car was started, I reached out, resting my hand on his thigh.

He let out a shuddering breath, spreading his legs and wiggling down a little so that my hand slipped higher.

I chuckled, giving him what he wanted because I could not resist.

I withdrew only long enough to pull out of the spot, then slid my palm over the hard bulge in his pants, letting it rest there the moment I pulled onto the road.

He moaned softly, his own hand dropping on top of mine, encouraging me to move.

I rubbed him slowly, feeling him twitch under all that fabric.

When I glanced away from the road, his head was back and he was watching me. He looked so hot and horny that I nearly choked on air.

"Fuck," I breathed, "you're so sexy, Jaime."

"I want to make you come this time," he said and really, I had no intention of stopping it this time, but now that he'd said that, I'd just have to bend over backward to give it to him however he wanted.

"Yeah?"

He nodded eagerly.

"What do you want to do?"

"Suck you," he whispered. Like it was something he shouldn't want. This was still new to him, I reminded myself, and lifted my hand from where it was rubbing his cock languidly, to slide it against the back of his neck, comforting and commanding at once. His eyes fluttered shut.

"Now?" I asked.

His gaze shot open and he glanced around at the road. We were at a stop sign heading through Gaynor Village. The area was relatively quiet and Gaynor Heights would be even more so once we got into my neighborhood. But I didn't want to force him; I'd just thought that was what he wanted and I wasn't about to argue with that.

I opened my mouth to tell him it could wait, but suddenly, he was diving down, pressing his face into my lap.

I gasped, reaching down and sliding the seat back far enough that I could still drive as he promptly unzipped me and pulled my throbbing cock free.

His hand was loose and confident around my base, but he didn't move for a moment.

"What's wrong?" I asked.

If he was self-conscious, there was no need. I was already in danger of precome leaking and he was barely touching me. The lead-up had been too much. Then again, I could barely even remember the first time I'd sucked cock. High school had been a bit of a whirlwind for me, but I'd known I was gay, had seen plenty of porn, had time to imagine it.

"Kiss my tip," I ordered.

Jaime sagged with relief and his gorgeous full lips

pressed to my tip, kissing it chastely, almost shyly for a second before he warmed up.

When he added his tongue in, my eyelids nearly fluttered shut.

I had to remind myself that I was still driving, forcing my eyes on the road and concentrating on that. It helped to not completely lose it when he started to experiment more, pressing the tip of his tongue against the slit and sucking the head into his mouth, swirling his tongue around it.

Thankfully, we were so close to my home that I was pulling in before he decided to try to suck me down any further.

He didn't seem to notice that we'd stopped, and I didn't bother telling him because my brain promptly turned to mush. In the dark of the car, with the soft sounds of his lips and tongue on my flesh, all I could do was lean back and luxuriate in the sensations until I needed more.

"Okay, slide it all the way in," I whispered. "And suck."

He did at once, taking me deeper than he could and choking a little before he drew back to a more comfortable position.

He sucked hard, lips pressed around me tightly and my eyes rolled, a hand tangling into his long hair, gripping him and holding him in place.

"Up," I groaned, pulling him close to the tip. "Keep sucking baby."

He moaned in response, letting me direct his head up and down slowly. When he choked again, I released him, letting him up for air. He only took a moment, barely lifting to gulp in air before diving back down and sucking me eagerly back into his wet heat.

"Use your tongue too," I grit out.

He did at once, tonguing my shaft while he bobbed, lips closed tightly around me.

It took everything in me not to thrust up. But I didn't need to. He was doing a good job. It felt amazing.

"I'm going to come soon," I said, stroking the nape of his neck.

He groaned in eager anticipation.

I reached for his lap, feeling his hard cock again. The front of his pants were wet now and when I squeezed, he bucked, gasping.

Immediately, he sucked my cock down again with renewed vigor, moaning even more loudly.

I let out a shuddering groan. My hands were shaking now, one gripping the wheel too hard, the other in his hair again clenching just as tightly.

"Listen," I said, shuddering. "Slide my cock in as far as you can. Keep sucking. When I start coming, suck it down, okay? Just swallow it as it comes out."

He groaned and slid me in deep.

"Fuck," I groaned as he followed my instructions. "Yes. Jaime, that's fucking perfect. I'm going to come."

The first spurts of release had me arching back, my hips thrusting up off the seat while I accidentally held his head down.

When he started to choke, I released him at once, clasping the wheel with both hands instead while he swallowed, moaning obscenely.

"Keep swallowing," I moaned, riding out the last of it, my tip pressed to the back of his throat as he did.

When the last of the pulsing throbs ran through my length and my balls, I collapsed back, ears ringing.

Jaime didn't lift off right away. He gave me another

slow, gentle suck that was almost too much as he pulled off, then kissed the wet tip softly.

"Jesus Christ," I muttered as he lifted up. I wished there was more light out here. I wanted to see the look on his face. Instead, I slid my hand into his hair and tugged him toward me for a deep kiss.

His lips were puffy and tasted like come.

"That was incredible," I whispered against his mouth.

He let out a shuddering breath and reached down, squeezing himself.

"Because you were telling me what to do," he groaned. "That was so fucking sexy."

Suddenly, he seemed to notice that my hands weren't on the wheel and glanced around.

"Oh. We're at your place."

"Yeah, I hope that's okay. I don't want any interruptions."

Jaime shivered.

"That's more than okay."

CHAPTER 13

JAIME

I DIDN'T KNOW WHAT ETHAN HAD IN STORE FOR ME, BUT AT this point, I knew I would do absolutely anything he wanted. It went beyond wanting him, and there was no doubt there that I did. But I trusted him too. Ethan seemed to be hardwired to me. He knew instinctively what I would like. Even things I didn't know I would like, he seemed crystal clear on.

The way he'd fingered me alone had gotten me hard for days every time I remembered it. Now, that blowjob would forever be in my memory bank, his gruff masculine voice and hard grip in my hair, the taste of him and his delicious musk. Who knew sucking cock could be so satisfying?

If not for the fact that a hard breeze would be enough to make me come in my pants right now, I would want to do it again. Maybe in the morning, he would let me do it again... I didn't know how that would work exactly, only that I hoped we wouldn't just fuck and then say goodbye for the night.

I didn't need to worry about that for now though,

because being with Ethan was like being put in a warm bath. It erased every worry from my mind and made me feel at ease and hot and bothered at the same time.

He unlocked the door, then stood back for me to enter ahead of him.

The entry way was large, with a built-in bench and hardwood floors that ran into the rest of the house. To the left, the living room was large, with a big fireplace and a comfortable-looking couch. There were guitars hanging on the walls and big windows. I could see it opened up into an equally impressive kitchen, currently shrouded in darkness. Straight ahead, a large staircase led to the second floor.

Before I could take in much more than that, Ethan's arms came around my waist, pulling me tightly to his hard chest.

I leaned into him, allowing my eyes to drift shut as he rocked me for a moment.

"See, what you did back there was a bad idea for you."

I frowned.

"How so?"

"Well, now I'm not in a rush to get off again," he whispered, pressing a kiss to my earlobe. "I can take my time on you... I can keep you hanging on all night if I want to."

I shivered.

My cock was already screaming for release. It was borderline uncomfortable, but his words sent a thrill through me. The idea of him keeping me on edge for hours, making me come apart entirely sent a fresh wave of pleasure through me.

"Mm," he moaned, holding me tighter, "it seems like you like that idea."

I swallowed, still couldn't find a word to say, and simply nodded.

"Upstairs," he said, releasing me.

We made it to his bedroom in record time. Ethan flicked on the bedside lamp and I had enough time to look around, take in the large area curtained off for the window, the door that lead to an ensuite, and his king-size bed before I realized he was pulling his clothes off.

His shirt hit the floor and his eyes met mine as he started to undo his pants.

He pushed them down, and I was finally able to see what I'd had in my mouth minutes ago. His cock lay limp and heavy between lean, muscular thighs. His narrow hips and the whisper of hair down his legs and over his firm chest made my stomach somersault with want.

"What do you think?" he asked.

The confidence in his voice and the smirk on his face suggested that he could already tell what I thought, but I lifted my chin and answered.

"You're really hot," I said honestly.

"Yeah?" he asked taking a step toward me. "Let me see you now."

I let out a breathy laugh.

"You already saw me naked."

He chuckled, reaching for my jeans while I pulled my shirt over my head.

"I want to see you again."

He pushed my pants down, letting out a breath when my cock sprang free.

I looked down at the obscene sight, flushed with blood and wet with precome.

Ethan groaned.

"Looks like you need some help with that, right now."

He reached down, wrapping a hand around my length and giving me a long slow push that made my toes curl.

I shuddered, wrapping my arms around his shoulders for support as he kept going.

His arm went around my waist, offering more stability while his speed increased.

His lips found my neck, sucking and biting while he jerked me.

"I'm going to come," I gasped, unable and unwilling to hold it in any longer.

He bit down on my shoulder, sucking the skin between his lips, but didn't stop or slow down.

Just as my balls tightened, ready for release, he suddenly let go.

I gasped, hips jerking after him automatically as a bit of come splashed from the tip.

He let out a deep moan but didn't grip my cock again. When an embarrassingly desperate noise left my throat, he gripped me by the hips with his strong hands and steered me toward the bed.

"Ethan," I gasped. "What the hell?"

He pressed his forehead to mine, gaze serious.

"I told you I was going to make you last as long as I could, didn't I?"

Suddenly his words from before seemed more foreboding. Still, my heart raced with excitement.

He pushed me back gently.

"Lay down baby, spread out."

Hands and knees shaking, I crawled onto his bed, getting to the pillows before lying flat on my back, spreading my legs like he wanted me to.

"Grab onto the railing," Ethan instructed.

He was pulling his shaft now. It was half hard again and looked almost as big as it had felt in my mouth.

I reached up, gripping the cold metal as he climbed onto the bed, kneeling between my legs.

Fuck, he was a sight perched there, his cock in his hand and mine left neglected in front of him.

Finally, he released himself, and reached down, hooking his hands under my knees and lifting them so that my feet were perched on the mattress.

"You look so good," he said, stroking my thighs. "I love having you here."

My hips lifted, despite myself.

Smirking, he pressed me flat to the bed, carefully not touching my cock.

His hands traced lower, skating over my balls and taint before circling my hole.

I clenched in anticipation, but he moved his hand away, bending down instead. Before I could process what he was about to do, his tongue was on me, licking with long strokes before plunging in.

I gasped, pulling away at the strange sensation. He didn't let me go far, gripping my hips and pulling me back down to meet his mouth as he started again, kissing me down there until I wasn't sure it felt weird anymore.

My entire body was hot. My cock felt useless, twitching and aching between us while he speared me repeatedly with his tongue, moaning in pleasure. When he swirled his tongue around, stretching me out, all I could do was hang on tight and ride the wave as it turned into intense pleasure.

I groaned, pressing down, suddenly desperate for more.

Almost immediately, something thicker entered me. I

gasped, looking down to see the way Ethan's arm pumped as he fingered me, his tongue still just inside, alongside the digit. When he slid another finger inside, he lifted enough to see my face, slowly shaking his head.

"Damn," he whispered, "you're so cute like this."

I was powerless to answer, clinging to the metal headboard and looking at him while my cock wept and soft keening noises were pulled out of me.

My thighs were shaking, cock bobbing every time his fingers thrust against my prostate. If it was possible, I thought I might come if he kept doing that. I was so close that even the heat of his breath would get me there if he tried that thing from the last time again.

He was fully hard now and so much bigger than I'd realized he was. In the car, sitting with so little room, I clearly hadn't realized just how much was still buried in the flaps of his boxers. No wonder he walked around with so much confidence.

Ethan caught me watching it and his free hand went down, clasping his length.

"You ready for all this, Jaime?" he asked.

I didn't know but I found myself nodding.

He let out a shaky breath, releasing me.

I cried out in disappointment, reaching for him but he braced himself over me, taking a moment to press a kiss to my lips when our eyes met.

"Just a second, love," he whispered, reaching into his bedside table.

He came back with lube and a condom. He sat back, rolled it on, then poured the liquid straight onto his hard length.

He shifted, positioning himself, and nerves had me suddenly clenching on air to keep him out. I couldn't take that. Two fingers had felt like enough. That amount of stretch and stimulation had felt good. Something told me his massive cock would hurt like hell.

Ethan seemed to see it all happen. He smiled, gaze fixed on my hole and ran his fingers over it again, teasing me until I started to relax again. When I did, he pressed them inside, letting me feel the delicious rhythm all over again as he bent over me, kissing my stomach, then my ribs. He settled on my nipples, biting them while he pleasured me.

Without realizing it, I'd let go of the bed and was now clinging to his shoulders. He felt so firm and stable. My knees clamped around his hips, keeping him there.

Groaning, Ethan pulled his hand free, sliding up so that we were chest to chest.

He kissed me deeply and I returned it, falling into the feeling of him over me, his body slick with sweat, my cock finally getting some relief from being pressed to his abdomen.

"It'll feel even better than my fingers," he promised, biting gently into my bottom lip as his tip pressed to my entrance.

Before I could decide if I believed him, my loosened hole took his tip.

I gasped, nails digging into his back, my entire body stiffening at the sudden breach. I seemed to have no control over the way my hole clenched around him in a death grip.

He inhaled sharply, remaining very still.

"Breathe, baby," he reminded me and pressed kisses all over my face, distracting me when he got to my lips again and started to kiss me.

The moment I started to loosen, he pushed forward,

sliding in deeper. I clenched instinctively again, my body trying to stop him but he went as deep as he needed to, rearranging my insides before stilling.

"Fuck," I gasped, "I thought you said this was supposed to feel good."

Regret filled his gaze. I instantly wished I could take the words back, but I was uncomfortable, stretched too wide and it stung and felt like I was being impaled at the same time. I didn't think I could move. I definitely didn't think he would be able to fuck me, but he seemed determined to keep going, slowly canting his hips back, then pressing them in deep again.

I breathed, clutching his shoulders, staring into his eyes and watching the pleasure intensify in them and that was enough to change everything.

I tipped my chin, catching his lips with mine, letting them brush together sensually. His eyes fluttered and suddenly, it didn't feel so bad anymore.

With the next thrust, it felt kind of okay. I could clearly enjoy anal stuff. Everything he'd done to me so far was enough to make me pop. I wanted to like this just as much. Anything that made Ethan's eyes lose focus and roll like that had to be good.

Taking a steadying breath, I braced my feet on the bed and moved my hips around, trying to find a good angle.

Ethan bit his lip, stilling while I did.

"You want a better angle?" he asked.

"Yeah."

Swallowing, he pushed up, forcing me to release him as he sat back, cock still buried deep in my ass.

The angle instantly stretched me out more. It made him feel even thicker. Everything was more intense.

I gasped, hands gripping the blanket as sharp tendrils

of pleasure shot through me, just like when he fingered me.

"Better?" He asked, stroking my inner thighs.

I nodded eagerly.

"Yeah, like that."

He groaned, taking that as permission to stop holding back. Gripping my thighs, he pulled me onto his lap better and started to fuck me with quick thrusts.

This position was better in another way. We got to watch each other. I got to see the look on Ethan's face, the sexy way his lips parted, the sensual way he moved, his hips rolling into *me*. I couldn't believe it. I was getting fucked by the guy I watched on TV. A week ago I'd thought I was straight and we didn't even know each other. Thank god I'd gone crazy enough to go to that reading because Ethan suddenly felt incredible inside me.

"Fuck," I gasped, desperately reaching for my knees and pulling them to my chest in an effort to get him in deeper.

He let out a low growl and leaned over me, bracing his arms on each side.

"You want more baby?" he asked. "You want me to fuck you deeper? Can you handle it?"

My jaw dropped. Partially because at this angle, with him continuing to fuck me I thought I was going to explode. Partially because of his question.

"You mean you're not in all the way?" I gasped.

I got my answer when he smirked.

"You're only taking about half right now," he informed me, slowing the roll of his hips, drawing out the way his thick cock dug into my prostate until I was leaking.

I moaned, arching off the bed, following his hips as they retreated.

Luckily, he seemed to guess my answer and pressed forward. I cried out but he didn't stop until he was balls deep, his cock throbbing within me.

He groaned deeply, resting his head on my shoulder, breathing heavily while he gave me a minute to adjust. Then, he hooked under my knees with his elbows and gave a long, truly deep thrust that made my eyes roll.

I gripped his shoulders, hanging on for dear life while he started to go harder and faster, consistently dragging cries of pleasure from me until I arched off the bed.

The force of my release was stronger than any orgasm I could remember having. Everything all at once was almost too much. Ethan's cock rammed into me, sliding in and out while my muscles flexed around him, my cock jammed between us, his grunts of pleasure in my ear, the slick feel of his skin, all of it was too intense.

It seemed to go on longer than any orgasm I'd ever had, my cock jerking between us, toes curling.

By the time it was done, my ears were ringing and I didn't think I could move.

Ethan was still fucking me. He had a grip on my shoulders and was using that as leverage to thrust into me. His entire body was shaking with the effort and I let him, surprised to still be enjoying the feeling of him inside me until with a last, body-wracking shudder, he came.

I shut my eyes, soaking in the feeling of his length flexing within me. Too bad I didn't get to feel his come too. For some reason, I wanted to. I wanted to know what it felt like spilling deep within me.

With a heavy, satisfied moan, he let his weight fall completely on top of me.

We were both breathing heavily, his cock was still

inside me, sweat drying on our skin but I didn't think I'd ever felt so comfortable.

My arms went around his back, hands gently stroking his cooling skin.

"Thank you," I found myself whispering.

He moaned contentedly.

"I should be thanking you, Jaime. You're amazing."

He wiggled his hips with a happy sigh, still not sliding out of me. I didn't want him to. I wanted to stay just like this.

Hoping he'd get the idea, I wrapped my legs around his hips, keeping him where he was. Like a delightful, sexy, weighted blanket made just for me.

CHAPTER 14

ETHAN

ALMOST IMMEDIATELY, JAIME'S ARMS GREW HEAVY ON MY back and his breathing evened. The gentle rise and fall of his chest under me nearly lulled me after him, but I could only imagine how Naomi would react if we left her watching Evie for the entire night.

She thought we were just going for dinner after all, and my phone was god-knew where, so I couldn't even ask.

Sighing, I snuggled closer to Jaime, pressing my face to his neck, inhaling the warmth of his scent.

Everything about him called to me in a way I was unfamiliar with. He was beautiful. Not just in appearance either.

I moved my hips a little, feeling his heat still around my cock. Why the hell did everything about him feel like home? I barely knew Jaime, yet I never wanted to leave his embrace. His arms and legs around me made me feel like I was exactly where I was meant to be, for the first time.

I'd always forced myself into the places I wanted. I'd had to carve myself into the show I now had, to seek out agents and publishers and artists for my books. I was proud of myself, but as of yet, nothing had ever just fallen into place like this. There had always been trial and error first. I would do everything I could to preserve and hold onto this thing forming between us.

I allowed myself another minute to relish in Jamie's embrace before waking him.

"All right, sweetheart, it's time to get up."

Jamie didn't even twitch.

"Jamie. Come on, beautiful." I pressed a kiss to his smooth cheek, then one to his lips. "Evie needs you."

That finally got Jamie's attention. His eyes flew open in sleepy confusion.

"Hm? What happened to Evie?"

He tried to get up, but I held him down, feeling the way his heart started to pound.

"Sh. It's okay." I stroked back his hair soothingly as he blinked fully awake. "Nothing happened. We just can't sleep here. Got to get back to your baby girl."

The tension melted from his body and he let out a sigh of relief.

"Oh. Right."

"Yeah," I whispered, pressing our lips together again.

He sighed again, a happy, contented sigh as our bodies melted together again.

"This is so nice," he whispered.

"It's the best," I agreed, smiling softly. "I hate to have to ruin it."

"We could always continue at my place," he suggested, suddenly not meeting my gaze.

My heart gave a happy little skip.

"You want me to stay the night?" I asked.

He bit his lip, nodding.

So sweet.

I placed my hands on his cheeks, steering him to look at me again.

"I would love that," I said firmly.

He smiled happily, his fingers sliding into my hair to pull me in for a soft kiss. It deepened languidly, tongues slipping out to meet each other. Relaxed and warm, just connecting on another level.

Grudgingly, I slid my hips back, freeing my cock from the welcoming heat of his hole.

Jamie gasped softly, pulling back with a frown and wiggling his hips.

"Oh, that feels weird now."

The fact that, at that moment, keeping me inside had turned into something that felt more natural than being without me was strangely beautiful.

I pulled him in tightly, giving him one last squeeze.

"Come on," I said, forcing myself to stand before turning back to look at him.

Jaime was spread out, loose, with come dried all over his abdomen. He looked fucking delicious but not fit for travel.

Glancing down at myself, I looked even worse with a condom hanging precariously off my tip.

I grabbed it hastily, tying it off.

"Okay. Showers first," I chuckled.

Jaime grinned.

"Together?"

I laughed, offering him my hand.

"Only if we promise to keep our hands off of each other."

Jaime took my hand, letting me help him out of bed.

I should have known that it would be impossible.

We managed to get under the hot spray without getting

into anything, but the moment we started to slide soapy hands over each other, Jaime's cock stood to attention.

Probably my fault, dragging him along like that for so long and only letting him come once. Next time, I'd see how many orgasms I could milk out of him. My cock grew heavy with interest, but I had already come twice in a short enough span of time.

Jaime didn't seem to mind though, especially when I wrapped an arm around his waist and took him in my hand, jerking him off with a slippery lather of soap, leaving his swollen asshole alone this time.

His come washed away with the spray as soon as it splattered from the tip, leaving him even more pliant and relaxed in my arms.

"Mm," I sighed, holding him tight to my chest under the warmth of the water. "Naomi is going to be so pissed."

He chuckled.

"Okay, let's get going then. I do want to check on Evie."

———

NAOMI WAS SPRAWLED ON THE COUCH, WATCHING REALITY TV when we entered.

"Well, hello!" she said. "How was your date?"

"Great," I said. "How was Evie?"

"A bit upset at first. I think she missed her daddy, but she calmed down. She's asleep in her bed now."

"That's good," Jaime said. "Thank you."

She nodded.

"Of course."

Jaime glanced at me.

"I'm just going to check on her."

I waved him off and Naomi stood, stretching.

"Sorry we took a while," I said, self-conscious despite the fact that she didn't seem too bothered.

"Hm? You're fine. You were only gone for..." She lifted her phone checked the time and paused. "Over three and a half hours. Okay."

She gave me an amused look.

"I'm guessing you did more than dinner."

I shrugged.

"Yeah, well..."

She smacked my arm, playfully.

"Ethan, you dog. No wonder the boys are always chasing you."

I chuckled.

"Please shut up before Jaime hears you."

She grinned and pulled on her jacket.

"So, it was good then?" she asked.

I nodded, biting my lip to stop from overspilling.

"So good. I *really* like him. Hoping you do too..."

She gave me a warm smile.

"Hey, it's your love life. My opinion doesn't matter. But, if this is about my concerns from before..." She shrugged. "I trust your judgment and he does seem really sweet once you get past the moody exterior."

I'd completely forgotten he came across that way at first.

"He's just shy," I argued, lowering my voice. "Maybe a bit insecure too."

She nodded thoughtfully.

"I could see that. Anyway," she said, kicking on her shoes, "say goodnight for me, okay? I'll leave you guys to it. And also, Evie is a pretty chill baby. She's mild-mannered and very sweet. He lucked out."

"She is adorable, isn't she?"

"A hundred percent. You'll make good co-parents."

"Hey," I said, smacking her.

She laughed, gave me a wink, and wished me goodnight.

I knew it was only meant to be a teasing joke, but the idea of it, of being Evie's dad, sharing my home and my life with both her and Jaime, made me feel *excitement*.

Speaking of Jaime…

I kicked off my shoes and hung my coat on the hook before going to the bedroom.

Jaime was standing over the crib, watching Evie. The light from the hallway was enough to see the soft look on his face.

When I stepped up next to him, he immediately leaned against me.

I put an arm around his shoulder, holding him.

"She looks so peaceful," he said quietly.

I looked down at Evie. She did indeed, in a fuzzy onesie, her face turned to the side, chest rising and falling softly.

"I left for hours and she's just fine."

"Yeah," I agreed, kissing the top of his head. "How does that feel?"

"Surreal," he said. "In a good way. Like I don't need to worry as much. For a while, if I wasn't physically *touching* her, I would panic."

"Did you think she would get hurt?" I asked gently.

"Yes," he whispered. "She's so delicate… I just wanted to protect her."

"You did," I whispered, stroking back his hair. "You were there for her when no one else could be."

Jaime took a shuddering breath.

"And you were there for *me* when no one else could be. I can't tell you how much that means to me."

I could hear the emotion in his voice and pulled him into a tight embrace, unsure of what else to do.

He clung to me, and I could feel the way his breath trembled.

"Come to bed," I whispered.

He nodded, pulling off his clothes but for his boxers and climbing in. I joined him, getting into the cool sheets and wrapping him up in my arms.

"Everything's okay now," I found myself whispering into his hair.

CHAPTER 15

JAIME

As expected, Evie woke up in the middle of the night for a feed and a diaper change. At the sound of her crying, I got up instinctively, before I was even fully awake.

It only took a minute to get her clean and then I couldn't resist climbing back into bed with her in my arms.

Ethan was awake, watching with sleep-hazed eyes.

He held the blanket up for me, tucking it around me when I settled down, Evie cradled in my arm and bottle held to her lips.

I never would have dared to do this before. It still made me a little bit nervous, but people co-slept all the time, and Ethan holding me where I was made me a little bit more comfortable.

It felt like I'd fallen into a little slice of heaven here in my small apartment. Cuddled up with both of the people I loved.

The thought just flew into my mind unbidden. I stiffened momentarily, then let the shock and fear go. It was the middle of the night. Maybe I'd fallen in love with

Ethan a little too fast, but I could deal with that in the morning. He was here now.

Sighing, I sank into the pillow, relishing the cute sounds Evie made while she drank her bottle, half asleep.

I woke up sometime later with the bottle laying on its side, dripping onto the mattress and Evie passed out, still on my shoulder. Behind me, Ethan was snoring softly.

Nothing had happened, but I had to take baby steps here. I couldn't bring myself to go back to sleep with Evie in bed with me. Just in case.

As carefully as I could, I lifted her and crawled out of bed.

She let out a little disgruntled noise, but I held her still, rocking her until she was snoring again, then carefully laid her back down in her crib.

Satisfied, I moved her bottle to the bedside table and crawled back into bed.

This was how nights were with a baby. Constantly interrupted, but also filled with snuggles, so how could I complain? Especially when Ethan pulled me into his arms in his sleep, nuzzling my hair with a sigh.

When I woke again, the sun was starting to come in under the blackout curtains and Ethan was awake, leaning on an elbow, watching me, his fingers gently brushing through my hair.

"Morning," he said softly, giving me a heart-melting smile.

"Morning," I whispered. "How long have you been up?"

"A bit," he said, fingers touching my jaw now. "Just thinking about how wonderful you are."

I blushed and tried to turn away, but he tilted my face back toward his for a soft, lingering kiss.

"I was thinking that I could help you with some of your list," he said, drawing back.

I blinked.

"You want to take the driving test for me?" I asked at once.

He grinned.

"No. But maybe I can help you find a daycare? Then you'll have time for the driving training… or I could teach you, if you want? I don't mind."

The idea of Ethan seeing me behind the wheel made me shudder.

"Maybe I'll start with GED classes," I mused. "We can put the driving last."

He raised a brow.

"You have your learner's, right?" At my nod, he went on. "With a child, that's probably the first thing you should sort out."

I stiffened.

"Okay, well, I'll think about it. It'll be fine. I'll figure it out."

This conversation was steering far too close to arguments I'd had with my father and sister on one too many occasions. I'd only gotten the learner's to shut them up. It had worked for a while. But now I knew I really did need to get over my fear.

Ethan was watching me closely. I waited for him to push it, but after a moment, he just smiled and kissed me.

Suddenly Evie began to coo, nearly reducing me into a puddle at the cuteness.

"Aw," Ethan said, smiling. "How adorable."

We listened silently for a minute and then the need for the bathroom won out.

"I'll be right back," I said.

He nodded, pecking my cheek before letting me go.

"Morning baby," I said to Evie, taking a minute to touch her little cheek before I went to the washroom.

It felt downright luxurious waking up like this, Ethan in my bed, snuggling and talking about the future, Evie happy as could be in the room with us.

My body felt a bit off from the sex: my thighs felt like they'd had a hard workout and when I sat down on the toilet seat, I couldn't resist slipping my fingers down to feel the swollen edges of my hole.

For some reason, even *that* was satisfying. It was like a little souvenir. Proof of how much Ethan had stretched me out with his thick cock.

I swallowed as it hit me again.

I'd let a guy fuck me, and it had been so unexpectedly good. With Ethan, anything would be amazing, I was sure. Hell, if he wanted to sniff feet and have golden showers, I wouldn't even argue at this point. He instinctively seemed to know what I would like, even when I didn't know.

Still, the thought made me crinkle my nose a little. Hopefully, he *didn't* like golden showers.

Since Ethan was there and I didn't feel like I had to run back out there, I took my time washing my face and brushing my teeth. When I finally emerged, the sound of someone clanking around the kitchen drew my attention.

I followed the noises, stopping in the doorway to see Ethan, with Evie strapped to his chest, moving around the place. Coffee was already brewing as he opened another cupboard.

"Now, where does your daddy keep the pans?" he asked Evie.

"Bottom cupboard on the right of the stove," I said.

He glanced over at me, grinning.

"She might need to be fed soon," he said. "But I think she's happy enough for now."

I nodded, taking a seat at the table, and watching as Ethan went to work making eggs.

"There's bacon too," I informed him, taking advantage of getting a meal cooked for me.

"Say no more," he said, going to the fridge and rifling through it.

I sat back, watching, a smile plastered to my face.

Of course, the moment the food was placed on the table, Evie started fussing and gesturing for her bottle by bringing her little hands to her puckered lips.

"Aw, bad timing," I chuckled, but before I could fully stand, Ethan was on his feet again.

"No, you sit. You were up with her for half the night."

Compared to before, being woken up twice was nothing. Still, I appreciated the gesture. Since there was milk already made in the fridge, it only took Ethan a couple minutes to have it warm and ready. He came back, taking his seat across from me while me and Evie ate.

I watched while he looked down at her, warmth and something like sadness in his gaze.

"She's so adorable," he said softly, so I guessed I was misreading him. Why would looking at a baby make anyone sad?

"Do you want to come to the mall with us?" I asked. "I need to get her new clothes. Or we could go for a walk?"

"How about both?" Ethan suggested.

I smiled.

"Sure."

———

WE ENDED UP BACK AT WEST COAST SNUGGLES INSTEAD OF the mall and this time, I went almost as crazy as the first time, but with the clothes. All of the outfits were hard to resist. I could so clearly imagine little Evie in any of them. Then there were the shoes! The fact that they were even made so tiny was insane. She had none to begin with, so the next thing I knew, I had five pairs in the basket that would match the outfits I'd picked.

"I'm so excited to dress her!" I said as we left. "It's so weird."

"It's not," Ethan chuckled. "It's one of the perks. Until she's older, you get to decide."

I laughed.

"My mom insisted on a faux-hawk for me as a kid. Do you remember those?"

Ethan laughed.

"Oh yeah. Everyone had one."

"Did you?" I asked. "Oh man, teenage Ethan with a faux-hawk, I need to see pictures."

He shook his head.

"No. All pictures have been burned, I'm sorry."

Ethan tugged me toward a gelato shop, and I buzzed happily. It was one of the first properly nice days we'd had yet and it was a Saturday, so the shop was full. But Evie was being good, falling asleep and waking up to look around periodically. She seemed to like looking at bright colors, so I stood next to the pink and green menu, pointing it out to her while she stared in amazement.

"Everything is so exciting when you're a baby," I mused. "Even basic colors."

Ethan grinned and put an arm around my shoulders. My stomach erupted with butterflies.

Oh god, I hoped this was more than just a fling for him.

I swallowed and leaned against him, relishing the feeling of being next to him.

When we finally got our ice cream, Ethan released me, taking my hand instead while we began to stroll the downtown, looking in the windows we passed.

"So, your father left you money," Ethan said, steering back to business again. "It's obviously enough that you don't have to worry for now, but is it enough to get you through college and all that?"

I appreciated that he didn't ask how much it was. To him, he probably wouldn't think I had much at all. For me, it was more money than I would have dreamed of getting all in one go.

I licked my chocolate ice cream, considering.

"No. I'll need a job. Soon probably, so that I don't just spend everything I have."

He hummed thoughtfully.

"Maybe you should see a financial planner."

I shrugged. I hadn't thought about anything like that, but it did make sense.

"Do you mind if I ask you something?" Ethan asked.

He hadn't hesitated to ask me anything yet, so I slowed, wondering what could be so serious.

"Sure, what is it?"

"Why are you not into driving? Are you afraid?"

Even just the mention of me driving sent a cold chill through me. It often did if I wasn't prepared to talk about it.

For a moment, I wondered how to even phrase it. Then I realized that the only way he, or anyone, would understand would be to hear the whole story.

"Uh..." I struggled for words. "Because of my mom..."

My voice betrayed me with an unsteady wobble. The

moment it came out, Ethan stopped walking and placed a hand on my shoulder, squeezing gently.

Seventeen years later, but it didn't matter. It still seemed unfair.

"The driver wasn't even drunk or anything, just looking the wrong direction at a right-hand turn. Didn't realize it was her turn to cross and that was it. Our entire family was completely destroyed."

Ethan swallowed, watching me, his blue eyes filled with compassion.

"You seem to be doing okay now," he tried to argue, but I shook my head, years of painful memories rushing me.

"I'm trying, but..."

He took my free hand, pulling me toward a bench to sit down. I did, feeling silly for wanting to cry over something so old. It wasn't just that though.

"My dad—" I cleared my throat, then forced myself to speak. "He didn't handle it well. Her dying *or* being a single parent. He started drinking a lot. To be completely honest, we were neglected. Liz tried her best. She would make my lunches, but she was only nine and I usually went to school in dirty clothes. By the time she was fifteen, she was hooked on a couple different things."

I looked up at Ethan, wondering what he would think. Sympathy clouded his eyes.

"To be honest, I basically followed suit. Stopped going to school when I was sixteen."

"What did your dad have to say?" he asked gently.

I snorted.

"Honestly, I'm not sure he noticed. He just went to work, came home, and sat on the couch every day with his bottles... but I guess he kept the automatic life insurance payments going."

"How did he die?" Ethan asked.

"Liver failure," I said quietly.

Ethan looked away, his gaze falling somewhere across the street.

"Jesus," he finally said.

I chuckled humorlessly.

"Yeah."

For a long moment, silence dragged between us. I took the opportunity to toss the last of my ice cream into the bin next to us, not wanting it anymore. Ethan followed suit.

"All because Mom got hit by a car. Dad drank himself to death... Liz hasn't been able to pull herself out of that hole and I don't even blame her. It's so hard. She managed to get sober for a bit when she was pregnant, but then she fell right back in. You have to leave everything you're familiar with, the lifestyle, the friends..."

Ethan's hand found mine on the bench and he clasped it tightly.

"Jaime," he whispered. "Do you have any idea how strong you are?"

The tears I'd been successfully managing to hold back immediately stung my eyes.

I shook my head, turning away.

"You are," he insisted, and I could hear the conviction in his voice. "I can't imagine. I had all the support in the world. My dad was like a rock to me. My extended family did everything they could. Plus I had therapy, years of it, to deal with what happened to my mom."

I looked at him and saw the way he had to swallow down the pain, even now. My heart ached for him.

Ethan understood.

"What happened to her?" I asked in trepidation. No answer would be good enough. There was no reason in the world that would make losing a parent so young okay.

He took a shuddering breath.

"When I was four, she took my baby sister," he whispered, voice suddenly quavering, "and she drove into the bay with her."

Shock and horror ran through me in turns.

"Yeah," Ethan whispered at my expression. "I still don't know why I wasn't in that car with them."

I squeezed his hand tightly, at a loss for how to comfort him. What could I even say?

"When I saw you there that day, I don't know why it all came back to me."

And with that admission, Ethan's entry into my life suddenly shined in a different light.

CHAPTER 16

ETHAN

Jaime didn't say anything; he just scooted closer, frowning, and put his arms around me. I sank gratefully into his embrace, holding him close. Between us, Evie wiggled, and it was like catharsis. Something released within me, that no amount of therapy ever could.

Her small fists pressed to my chest, and I couldn't help but laugh, even though my voice shook.

"I know, sweetheart," I said, parting enough to look at her. "That was a long time ago. It's done now. We'll all be okay."

She looked up at me with those round blue eyes, so much like my sister's. I still remembered Amelia well. And the way she would always cry unless my mother was holding her. At the time, I'd even resented her because mom stopped looking at me. She only ever seemed to look at her.

I swallowed the memory down, surprised by how potent this all felt and how much it seemed like now that Jaime knew, I could finally move on. He had been my answer. My second chance. It didn't make any sense, yet here we were.

"Thank you," I whispered.

Jaime swallowed and shook his head.

"I don't know what to say."

"You don't have to say anything," I said.

I pressed my lips to his, surprised when he hesitated for a moment before returning the kiss.

"Let's head back," he said.

He stood first, and my stomach slowly knotted as I looked up at him. I'd said something wrong. I didn't know what exactly, but his shoulders were stiff and he was pointedly not looking at me.

When I stood up though, he immediately took my hand, easing some of my worries.

I could see his thoughts racing while we drove back to his place. His brown eyes were fixated out the window, even when Evie started to wail in the back.

"We're almost home, Evie," he said absently, but that was it.

I pulled in and let him take his time changing her, then settling into the armchair with her bottle.

When she was quietly sipping and the silence had gone on for too long, I finally couldn't hold myself back any longer.

"Are you going to tell me what's on your mind?"

Jaime didn't seem surprised by my question.

He took a long moment, gaze still fixed on Evie before he spoke.

"Did you really think I was going to hurt Evie?"

My stomach twisted into a knot.

Taking a slow breath, I slid across the couch cushions to be closer to the armchair where they were sitting.

"I don't know if I thought that specifically," I admitted. "But the way you were that day reminded me of how my mom was at that time."

He swallowed audibly.

"What way was that?"

"Stressed, lost... alone."

He gazed unseeing at the floor now, looking completely dejected. My heart ached, my mind scrambled for how to explain in such a way that he wouldn't hate me. I hadn't thought of how hurtful the comparison would be.

"You could tell that I felt alone just seeing me?" he asked, finally looking at me, pain in his eyes.

My silence answered his question. He squeezed his eyes shut, letting his head fall back onto the cushion.

"All this time, I just thought you were being nice and that maybe... you were even into me from the start." He laughed bitterly. "Turns out you just pitied me."

"Please don't think that," I whispered, aware of the way Evie's eyes were drooping sleepily. "It wasn't about you as much as it may seem like it was."

He gave me an incredulous look, and I shrugged awkwardly.

"Yeah, you reminded me of my mom a bit. And yeah, you looked tired and alone, but I put on shows for kids, Jaime. Not to mention two of my friends, Scott and Anthony, have *twins*. I see lots of tired parents. Something pushed me toward you two, specifically. Especially Evie... she looks a lot like Amelia did..."

I sighed, running a hand through my hair.

"I was only a child when they passed," I said softly. "I was completely helpless. I didn't even understand what was going on. I didn't get that parents had their own issues they were going through and needed to be helped too. Learning that has been a driving force for my entire life. Everything I've done—"

I swallowed back the emotions threatening.

Jaime watched me, pain and sympathy in his gaze while he waited for me to go on.

"Seeing you two, just made me want to *help* the way that I couldn't before."

Jaime's lips pursed. He looked down at Evie, shaking his head, and tears were suddenly in his eyes.

"I can't imagine what you've been through," he whispered.

I swallowed.

"Hey, I'm a grown man now... I'm okay. But apparently, I hadn't moved on quite as much as I'd thought because I couldn't resist checking in and doing what I could for you two." I smiled ruefully. "I mean, the fact that you're so easy on the eyes did help a little."

Jaime chuckled quietly, setting the bottle gently on the side table.

"Come with me to put her down," he said softly.

I stood, surprised, and followed Jaime to the bedroom.

He very carefully laid Evie into her crib and then straightened and turned to me, pressing into my arms for a deep embrace.

"You really forgive me?" I asked, pressing my lips to his hairline and breathing him in.

"There's nothing to forgive," he said gently, his hand stroking my back. "We're all human, right? We all get driven to do things based on our pasts. In this case, I hope..."

He drifted off, took a shuddering breath, but didn't seem able to speak.

"What is it, sweetheart?" I asked, rocking him.

His arms tightened around me, and he pressed his face into my neck before forcing the words out.

"I hope that being with me and Evie, seeing that we're okay, will help you to move on for real."

He lifted up, forcing himself to look at me through the tears in his brown eyes.

"What happened wasn't your fault. It wasn't up to you to fix anything or make her better."

He licked his lips and swallowed back more tears.

"I've been telling myself that for a long time about my dad and Liz too. Sometimes, you just have to do what's best for yourself."

Overcome, I stroked my thumbs over his cheeks, wiping quickly drying tears.

"How is it that, all these years later, what happened brought me to you."

"We must be meant for each other," he chuckled.

Warmth flooded me and I leaned forward, pressing our lips together, shocked that somehow, I'd found someone who truly felt me the way that I felt him.

CHAPTER 17

JAIME

THE INITIAL SHOCK OF ETHAN'S PAST HAD FADED INTO something warm and beautiful.

I didn't think I had ever felt so connected to someone. Whenever our eyes met, it felt like being wrapped in a blanket, and whenever he touched me was even better.

He didn't leave my place until Monday morning when he had to go in to work.

I tucked Evie's foot into the sparkly slippers I'd bought her. When our eyes met, she smiled... and I nearly screamed.

"Oh my god!" I hollered, lifted her into the air, and spun her around in my excitement. "Evie! That was so sweet!"

She let out a happy gargle and I held her out in front of me.

"One more time, baby! Give me another smile!"

She stared at me.

"Fine," I chuckled. "Be stubborn, just like Liz."

Still delighted, I tucked her into her carrier, facing out so that she could look around.

I zipped my jacket up halfway, grabbed my bag, and left into the bright April day.

I hadn't really noticed how many people smiled and said hi to Evie until today either. The general good vibes fed into my mood and determination. But first, I had to message Ethan.

We'd only been apart for a few hours. I knew he was filming for a while, but I still couldn't help feeling desperate to hear from him.

> Evie smiled at me!

Even typing the word felt surreal. She was growing so fast. I bent, kissing the top of her hat.

"Soon you'll be sitting up on your own," I said. It was the most basic skill, but hell, seeing her grow and get stronger was melting my heart already.

She seemed delighted to be out of the house. The bus ride kept her entertained with all the people and lights, but when I got to my destination, the nearest cafe, she was already asleep.

It was true that movement made it impossible for a baby to stay awake, I mused.

It worked for me though.

I ordered a coffee and settled down at a table, pulling out my laptop.

First order of business was one that would make me and Ethan the proudest.

My stomach squirmed while I found the local driving school, The Driving Academy. With a deep breath, I input my details and my card, ignoring the way it made my hands shake.

I was raising a child. I could handle anything.

That was what I told myself anyway. And Ethan had promised that if it was evening or weekend classes, he'd make himself available to watch Evie while I went to them.

Just taking that one step made me feel hugely accomplished. Even though it made my hands shake. I'd done it. I'd signed up and paid. That meant I would be driving soon.

Now, time to move on to another item on the list.

Suddenly my phone vibrated.

I pulled it out at once, eager for Ethan's message.

> That's amazing! I can't wait to see it!

> Also, I hope you don't mind, I contacted a daycare I found for you. I put your details though so they should be calling or emailing soon.

> I don't mind. That's perfect! Thank you.

Smiling, I crossed "find childcare" off my list.

That left getting my GED, deciding on a field of study, researching colleges and applying, and finding a job in the meantime.

It was all a little bit daunting, but I had a kid now and by the time she was on two feet, I wanted to know that I could care for her properly.

"One step at a time," I said to myself.

It turned out that there were night courses at the high school. But the idea of returning to Gaynor High at twenty-three made me feel a little bit sick. I'd been so glad to get the hell out of there.

But it would be different this time around, I decided. And for Evie, it would be worth it.

With that in mind, I began the application process.

Job hunting took much longer after that, updating my resume, and taking a break to play with Evie and feed her added, but at least I liked that part.

When my phone started to ring, I picked it up, surprised to see that a couple of hours had already passed.

"Where are you, babe?" Ethan asked. "I'm at your place, but no one's here."

"Oh, shit. I didn't know you were coming over."

"I kind of invited myself," he chuckled.

"I'm at Nice Buns," I said grinning.

"Can I join you?"

"Please do!"

My foot was tapping with anticipation while I waited for him. The moment he walked through the glass doors, my heart leaped.

I stood up to greet him with a kiss and a half hug since I was holding Evie in one arm.

"How was work?" I asked.

He groaned softly.

"Ugh. I'll tell you about it in a minute. Just let me grab a coffee."

He pecked my cheek before going to the front, his hand lingering on my back like he didn't want to stop touching me.

I sat back down, attempting to play it even a little bit cool, but catching his eyes twice when he turned to look at me.

He returned with a coffee and two muffins. He slid one over to me, smiling.

"What are you up to?" he asked.

I turned my computer toward him so he could see.

"Jobs," I said shrugging.

"Anything good?"

I shook my head.

"Not that I'm qualified for."

He grimaced.

"But I did set some other stuff up," I said, watching for his reaction. "GED classes and driving lessons. They even pick you up from home."

His brows shot up.

"Jaime!" He leaned across the table, pressing his lips to mine. "That's amazing. I'm so proud of you."

I chuckled, cheeks heating.

"Don't be too proud yet. I still have to pass them."

"You will," he said sincerely. "And once Tiny Tots daycare gets back to you, you won't have to rely on me to be free to babysit either. You'll have your days free again."

The idea of sending Evie off all day long made me squirm a little.

"Do they do half-days?" I asked uneasily.

"I'm sure there's some sort of part-time option," he said. "You can ask them when they get back to you."

I nodded, reminding myself to breathe. I would have to get used to not being glued to Evie if I was going to do all the things I planned for her.

"What about you?" I asked, remembering. "You said there was something you were going to tell me about your work?"

It still felt weird to refer to him filming his show as "work" even though that was what it was for Ethan. It was his regular day job, and his writing was his side hustle.

He grimaced and shook his head.

"It was a weird day," he said. "Some people came to watch the show getting filmed."

He took a sip of his coffee, his gaze drifting.

"Our ratings are really good and keep getting better… apparently we drew some attention from a big studio out in LA. Or maybe my producer Arty reached out to them, I'm not really sure."

I didn't know what to say for a moment, but the tentative way that Ethan was watching me made it all clear.

"They want to pick up your show?" I asked.

He nodded slowly.

"Yes. They're making some big promises. A bigger network and broader reach but… that would mean moving to LA."

"Oh."

"Yeah," he agreed, staring at me, clearly trying to read my reaction, and he must have seen something bad because he reached out, placing a hand over mine on the table.

"I didn't agree."

My eyes widened.

"What? Ethan, you have to!"

For a moment, he looked taken aback.

"But that would mean moving to LA," he repeated slowly, a flash of hurt crossing his eyes.

The way my heart leaped was probably the wrong reaction, but Ethan's meaning was clear. He didn't want me to want him to leave and that did something to me. It gave me something that I couldn't even express in words.

I turned my hand over, clasping his tightly in my own.

"I don't want you to go," I said slowly. "But it's such a good opportunity."

He shrugged, not meeting my gaze.

"It is. I just don't want to mess with this thing we have right now," he said with a heavy sigh.

I leaned across the table, holding back a smile.

Ethan met me halfway, pressing a kiss to my lips. The soft touch offered a quick reassurance. When I pulled back, Ethan looked more at ease.

"You don't have to decide right away, do you?" I asked. "Or maybe you can negotiate something and stay here?"

He shrugged.

"Maybe. They asked me to come see their studio on the weekend. Said they'd cover the flights. Maybe you two can come with me?"

I froze. For a moment, I felt debilitated, a million excuses rushing through me.

"Or not."

"I just registered for the driving courses that start this weekend," I rushed to explain. "Maybe I can cancel it."

The thought of the lessons themselves were enough to send me into a tailspin, but dealing with a trip to LA made it even worse. The idea of flying with an infant was awful; I didn't know how she would be on the plane. Then there was the matter of hotels, food, things to do, and places to see, all with a newborn. Would Ethan want a certain standard that I wouldn't be happy paying for? Would he try to cover for me? I didn't want him to feel pressured to pay for me. The idea of planning it all, let alone actually doing it, was nauseating.

"No, I'll only be gone for a couple days," Ethan said, squeezing my hand. "You do your class. It's important too."

I nodded, relief swamping me and then grimaced.

"Actually, I'll have to cancel it anyway. I was kind of banking on you babysitting."

"Ah. Shit, forgot about that part."

He dug his phone out of his pocket, typing a quick message.

"Hopefully Naomi is free."

It turned out that she was, and she was friendly and good with Evie, so I shouldn't have felt as weird about it as I did.

But I couldn't help the clawing unease I felt in my gut for the rest of the day.

CHAPTER 18

ETHAN

FOR THE DAYS THAT FOLLOWED THE OFFER, JAIME WAS CLINGY. He never seemed to want me to wander too far. He constantly wanted his hands on me and mine on him, even when it wasn't about sex.

I loved it.

Having the younger man's unabashed adoration gave me the type of confidence and fulfillment I used to dream of having. It made me feel excited about something other than my work, and I didn't think I had ever had that before. His presence, the domestic life I'd suddenly fallen into made me feel a sort of peaceful happiness. Especially in the small moments, when our eyes met over breakfast or I made him smile. Whenever he watched me play with or care for Evie, a tenderness filled his gaze that was enough to make my entire body tingle. Then there was being in bed with someone who completely trusted me, not just to bring him to release but to show him things about his own body he didn't know he liked. All of it felt special.

The night before my flight, as soon as Evie was passed

out in her crib, he came up behind me in the kitchen, wrapping his arms around my waist, his hard cock pressing into my ass cheek.

I set down the bottle I was washing, grinning when I turned to look at him and snaking an arm around his waist.

He grimaced.

"Your hands are getting my shirt wet."

"Well good thing you're not going to be wearing it for long."

He chuckled, stepping back and whipping it over his head while I grabbed the towel to dry my hands anyway.

"Couch?" I asked.

He nodded, rushing to the living room. Laughing, I followed, undoing my shirt on the way, blood rushing to my cock in anticipation.

By the time I got there, a moment after him, he was already laying back into the cushions, stark naked. He stretched his arms above his head, his entire body on display for me.

I let out a soft, hungry sound, quickly kicking out of my jeans to climb on top of him. His legs parted to make room for me, and I rolled my hips into the sweet space, meeting his cock with my own, allowing the lengths to drag together a couple of times before I leaned down and kissed his parted lips.

As soon as I did, he reached up, sliding his fingers into my hair, holding me there.

Reading him, I deepened the kiss, eager to satisfy his needs.

He arched up, his hips starting to move against mine, adding to the friction as our cocks slid together.

I'd been planning on something else, maybe bending

him over and fucking him silly, but that wasn't what he needed right now. And, it turned out, that wasn't what I needed either. I wanted this connection as much as he did.

With our faces close, lips sliding together, tongues tangling, there was no way to miss any moment. Even the smallest gasp or flicker of eyelashes was felt.

His cock felt incredible too, just like every part of him, hot, soft skin, muscles just underneath, and the perfect fit and size for me. It would almost make me think we were made to be together at moments like this.

Especially when his hips suddenly bucked, a moan tearing from his throat while precome gushed between us. He yanked my hips against his for more and my knees slipped, making me flop heavily on top of him, skin to skin from bottom to top, our cocks trapped in the wet heat of our bodies pinning them.

His breathing turned ragged, hands gripping my ass cheeks suddenly while he continued with renewed vigor.

Groaning, I met his thrusts, sliding my cock against his until we both started to shudder and move out of rhythm.

I couldn't say who came first—we both seemed to start spilling at the same time, making a hell of a mess that I had no desire to deal with just yet.

Jaime seemed to feel the same way because he hugged me to his chest, not letting me back up even long after he had caught his breath.

I pressed a kiss to his neck and then wiggled far enough to reach my fallen boxers. He grudgingly allowed me to pull far enough back to scrape some of the come off of our bellies. I wasn't going to like washing it out of the trail on my stomach later, but for the way Jaime quickly pulled me back into his embrace, it was worth it.

I maneuvered around until I was on my side, head next

to his on the arm rest, my arm hooked around his waist and leg draped possessively over both of his. He sighed, snuggling in closer.

With the way he was acting, I couldn't help feeling that he was a bit down. I'd hoped sex would cheer him up a bit, but he was lying there, silently, his eyes staring at the ceiling, his hand gripping my arm a little too tightly, like he thought I might run away.

"What's this tattoo about?" I asked, trying to draw his attention to something else.

"Hm?" He glanced down, seeing that I was tracing a finger over the small, somewhat crude shape of a snake on his bicep.

He grimaced.

"Ugh. A friend was learning. We were all drinking at his apartment and then he started offering free tattoos."

I raised an incredulous brow.

"You let someone tattoo you drunk?"

"Drunk me did, yes," he said, grinning. "Need to get it covered up, but it's kind of bumpy. Not sure I can hide it."

I ran my fingers over it again, feeling the soft, blister-like scar.

"It's not that bad," I said, then laughed at the look he gave me. "Okay, it is. But it's part of your story too. Nothing wrong with scars."

The moment the words left my mouth, the brightness in his eyes dimmed, and his lips twitched downwards.

"I'm going to miss you," he whispered.

I swallowed.

"I'll only be gone for two days," I reminded him.

He looked away.

"Yeah, I know."

Reaching up, I tilted his chin toward me, forcing him to meet my gaze.

"What are you afraid of?" I asked. "Do you not think I'm coming back on Sunday?"

"It's not that," he said softly.

Suddenly, without a word from him, I thought I understood. This was about me moving away. I was only going to LA to see about making the move permanent.

The idea of leaving Jaime behind made my entire body itch. I couldn't do it. But he didn't know that. And he wouldn't until I proved it to him.

I leaned in, pressing my lips to his.

He took the kiss desperately, pouring more emotion into the touch than I had ever felt and I met each fear he held with reassurance and confidence, trying to show him with my lips how much I was there to meet him halfway.

When we finally parted, his eyes were less scared.

"I'm not going to disappoint you," I whispered. "You'll see."

My words seemed to trouble him, making his brows draw lightly together before he let out a soft sigh and smiled.

"I know, Ethan," he said gently. "You're different."

I'd always strived to make a difference but never had I felt so fueled to be a better person and a better man than with this man in my arms.

No matter what my decision was, I didn't want to let Jaime down.

CHAPTER 19

JAIME

ETHAN WOKE ME UP WITH A KISS TO SAY GOODBYE IN THE morning. He was already dressed, smelling clean, his hair still damp, and scruff shaved.

"I have to head out to beat the traffic."

"Okay," I whispered sleepily.

He kissed me again while I stretched and somehow I managed not to fall into a depressed slump until after he was gone.

Ethan leaving was like the first stroke to the end. I knew that, despite whatever he told me.

I'd seen enough in life to not be much of an optimist.

First, he would go, see the amazing studio and life he could have in the big city. Then he would suggest something that wouldn't work, like long distance or commuting. We would drag this on for a bit longer if we were lucky. Then one of us would think it wasn't worth the effort and end it. And that would definitely be Ethan, because I was ready to cling to him until the bitter end.

Hours later, a knock on my door made me realize that I

was gazing blankly at the TV while it played random shows for toddlers.

Evie was chewing eagerly on a teether, propped up in the bouncer chair I'd bought her earlier in the week.

It still felt weird not to cart her everywhere with me the way I used to have to, even just to answer the door.

When I pulled it back, I stared at Naomi's round face and friendly smile for a long moment in confusion.

"Hi, Jaime, ready for your class?" she asked.

"Oh! Shit!"

She chuckled, entering when I held the door open for her.

"You need an assistant too," she remarked, kicking off her shoes and going to Evie. "Hello, sweetheart, remember me?"

Evie smiled and kicked, setting off a barrage of baby talk from Naomi.

I chuckled, listening to her telling Evie what a cute girl she was in a high-pitched voice while I went to the bedroom.

The sight of the unmade bed made me pause, remembering the feeling of being held warm in Ethan's arms only hours ago.

I shook myself, I had to stop being so dramatic. He was only going to be gone for the day. I could handle that. I had to focus on other things.

In particular, the lesson that I wasn't mentally prepared for.

Getting behind the wheel of a car had been too scary for me before. I'd nearly had a breakdown getting behind the wheel when Liz had insisted on showing me at seventeen, and never bothered trying again since.

But that was over five years ago now. I was a stronger

person now. I was a parent for god's sake. Nothing could be harder than that.

Taking a deep, calming breath, I changed out of my pajamas, into a clean outfit, and went back out to the living room.

"It's only supposed to be about thirty minutes," I said.

Naomi nodded.

"That's no problem."

Nodding, I went to Evie, kissing the top of her head.

"Be good to Naomi, okay?" I said.

There was a touch of chill in the air when I went outside, despite the blue sky. I hadn't pulled on my jacket, too preoccupied to think of it, but pulled my sweater close around my shoulders as I went to the front of the house.

"Oh! Jaime!"

I looked up, disappointed to find Mr. and Mrs. Woo sitting on the front porch in the sunlight, looking unbothered by the weather.

"Hi," I muttered.

"I want to talk to you about your daughter," Mrs. Woo said.

"Uh, sorry. I'm busy right now," I said, my heart instantly racing. What could they possibly have to say about her? What business was it of theirs? she was a quiet baby. I didn't think I'd read anything about the place not allowing children when I first moved in.

A silver car pulled up right at the end of the driveway with a sticker on the door that said The Driving Academy. That distracted from anything else that might be said.

Gratefully, I rushed to it, aware that the homeowners were still watching me.

Without thinking, I pulled open the passenger side door, jumping in.

"Oh. You must be Jaime?"

The driving instructor was a portly, middle-aged woman with thick-rimmed glasses. She looked totally unthreatening, but I still felt a wave of panic at the amused smile she gave me.

"Uh, yeah, I'm Jaime. Sorry."

"It's fine, hun. I'm your instructor, Magda. You're supposed to get in the driver's side though."

Duh, I thought. I could be so stupid sometimes.

"I'm sorry," I said, flushing with embarrassment.

"It's okay. You were so quick, I didn't even have a chance to get out," she laughed, opening her door.

I followed her lead, climbing out, face still red hot as we traded spots.

Suddenly, I was sitting behind the wheel. My entire body froze.

"Alright, click in your belt first," she said. "And I'll ask you a couple questions to begin."

Magda's easygoing voice helped a bit. She didn't seem worried at all.

"Have you driven at all yet? Or is this your first time?" she asked.

"Uh. First time," I choked.

"Okay, that's not a problem. Do you feel confident about the signs and rules?"

I nodded shakily.

"Alright, there's no need to be nervous. We'll take it nice and slow to start. Maybe we'll just go around the block."

She must have noticed the tension in my body, because she was speaking like I was a scared little animal, ready to bolt.

"To start, we have to take stock of everything around

us," she said.

For a few minutes, she showed me where I wanted the seat and mirrors to be positioned. Then she took her time explaining all the different functions, even the most basic ones, like the gas and brake pedals.

When she told me how to start the car though, everything changed.

It was like something had wrapped tight around my ribcage, slowly constricting me.

"Grab onto the wheel where I showed you," Magda said, not seeming to notice.

I did, trying to force air in. Just a few deep breaths would fix me. But I couldn't get them.

I threw open the door, in a sudden panic that escalated as I scrambled out of the car because I was suddenly sure that the gear wasn't set in park. I'd left her in the car and it was going to roll with no one even driving it.

I spun around and found the car sitting firmly in place, Magda watching me with wide eyes. Behind her, the Woos were standing on the porch now, not hiding their curiosity as I nearly fell to the pavement.

I had to grip the cold edges of the door frame and sink down to the rough road on my knees before any bit of sense seeped back into me.

In a strange, abstract kind of way, a very calm, disinterested voice told me to relax, that nothing bad was happening. I heard it, knowing that was true, but I was unable to do anything but wait for my vision to clear.

I didn't know how long it took, but when the spots started fading, Magda and the Woos were standing nearby, talking quietly.

I lifted my head, too tired to feel embarrassed.

"Here," Mr. Woo said, offering me a bottle of water.

I took it weakly, somehow managing to open it and take a sip.

"Sorry," I found myself muttering.

"Don't be sorry," Magda said genuinely. "A lot of people panic when it comes to driving."

I managed to get to my feet, but my whole body was shaking.

"I should be able to do this," I found myself saying.

"Some people never do," she said. "There's nothing wrong with that."

I swallowed.

"Can I reschedule?" I asked.

She smiled kindly.

"If that's what you would like, I'm happy to keep trying with you."

I nodded, shakily and pushed off the car.

Mr. Woo immediately came to help me. He was a lot quieter than his wife, and I was surprised by how insistent he was in walking me to my door. His wife followed, hurrying to open the door for us.

By the time I was inside and found Naomi bouncing Evie in her arms in the living room, I felt more humiliated than I could ever remember being.

"What happened?" she asked, her eyes wide, flying between us all.

"He had a panic attack," Mrs. Woo said.

"I'm going to lie down," I interrupted.

She nodded, still watching me with her eyes practically bugging out.

"Sure, take your time," she said, instantly more gentle after Mrs. Woo's words.

I made it to my bed, collapsing onto it. With the door

closed, I could still hear their voices, talking quietly, but not the words they were saying.

I waited until the living room was silent again, too afraid to show my face after what had happened.

When nearly an hour had passed, I finally forced myself up. I was still a little light-headed, but Naomi had originally agreed to babysit for half an hour and guilt was gnawing at me.

"Hey, how are you feeling?" she asked the moment I entered.

I shrugged dejectedly and she grimaced.

"I hope you don't mind that I ordered us Thai food for lunch."

I blinked, surprised.

"You didn't need to do that."

"Don't worry, it's on Ethan. I have a business expense card," she said, winking playfully.

I shook my head, an amused smile touching my lips as I sank down next to her on the couch. Evie was fast asleep in her bouncer on the cushion between us. I reached out, touching her little hand. Even in sleep, she gripped onto my finger tightly, soothing me.

"I can't seem to do anything without Ethan," I found myself muttering.

Naomi watched me with worried eyes.

"He seems to want to help," she said gently.

"I know," I sighed. "But it seems like I can't get through a day without taking something from him."

I couldn't believe I'd said it out loud, but once it was voiced and to his friend of all people, there was no taking it back.

"I need to be able to take care of myself properly. I don't want to keep needing him."

She frowned.

"So, you're not in this for the long haul?" she asked. "Because let me tell you, I've never seen Ethan like this about anyone before."

My stomach erupted with butterflies.

"I never want it to end!" I found myself defending. Her pleased look had me squeezing my eyes shut. "I just don't want him to feel like he's constantly taking care of me. I couldn't even take that car out of park."

"You know, that's not how it works between people who care about each other," she argued.

This time, I frowned.

"What do you mean?" I asked, confusion seeping into my voice.

"When you're having a hard time, you're *supposed* to lean on those who love you. Yeah, Ethan is your rock right now, but when it's his turn to need someone, you'll be there for him in."

I blinked, surprised. I hadn't thought of it that way. I certainly hadn't thought of Ethan *loving* me. He was so wonderful though that the idea was more than welcome. I'd meant what I'd said about wanting it to be forever.

But that didn't mean it would be. I had serious doubts that Ethan would choose me over taking his career to the next level. I wouldn't even want that for him. If I held him back in anyway, I'd never be able to forgive myself. Ethan had found his calling with his show and books. The way he'd made me feel when I was at my lowest was, in my opinion, proof that world needed him.

CHAPTER 20

ETHAN

LA WAS LIKE A DIFFERENT WORLD.

As I reached the outskirts of the city, the shocking skyline of skyscrapers, it was hard to believe that Gaynor Beach was under two hours away. Then I hit the morning traffic and remembered why I didn't visit very often.

I'd left early, but reaching the city before nine turned out to be a terrible idea.

Sighing, I resigned myself to move slowly while my mind wandered.

By the time I was parked and meeting studio execs about an hour later, I was wondering what the hell I was doing this for.

But then I saw the studio.

It was bustling with people, unlike the stage we booked in Gaynor. The whole place was filled with life.

"We film Moppet's Muppets here," the exec told me, walking me past their sound stage.

I slowed, taking it in, awed.

I'd often gained inspiration from the very puppet show

we were passing. The set was more intricate than I'd realized watching it on the TV.

He went on, listing the other shows filmed here for
their network, and by the end, my interest had taken a
complete turn.

This was better than I'd expected it to be. I would be
rubbing shoulders with other creatives in my industry,
feeding off of that energy. Meeting others who did what I
did was rare. Aside from the people who read at Gaynor
library, I didn't know many other children's entertainers.
That alone was an exciting prospect that I hadn't
thought of.

By the time I was sitting in an office, discussing business, the reach of their network, and the plans they had for
my show, I was beyond interested.

Money was a second thought, but then they presented
numbers and I nearly choked.

"Are you serious?" I asked. Then, before I could make
any mistakes, I shook myself. "This will have to go
through my agent."

They were the ones who knew how to negotiate, and I
wasn't about to dive into this headfirst on my own.

It wasn't until I found a nearby cafe for dinner that I
had a minute to properly catch my breath.

My head was swimming with options but when I sat
down and took a breath, I found my thoughts going
straight to Jaime.

He would be long done with his driving lesson already.
He'd been nervous, but now he was probably proud as
hell to have done it. I wished I'd been there to see that
excited look in his eyes.

I pulled my phone out, expecting a message from him.

Instead, there was one from Arty wishing me luck and a rather ominous text from Naomi.

Check in on your boy.

I stared.

That was it?

Heart racing, I dialed her number instead of texting back.

"What happened?" I demanded the moment I heard the line click.

She chuckled.

"Well, hello to you too," she said. "How was the meeting?"

"Really good. How is Jaime?"

"Not the best," she admitted. "He had a panic attack starting the car apparently. The neighbors walked him back in and he had to lie down…"

I didn't know what to say. The thought of that happening while I wasn't there just felt *wrong*.

"Ethan?"

"I'm here," I managed but I still couldn't find any words.

"Don't worry. He was okay after a while. I ordered lunch and stayed with him until he seemed better."

"Okay… So he's okay?"

She made a noncommittal sound.

"Kind of. He seems pretty down."

My heart sank.

"I should be there," I finally said, softly.

She sighed.

"Jaime seems to think you should be in LA moving on already."

I frowned.

"He said that?"

"Not in so many words," she said, clicking her tongue. "But the poor guy seems to be a bit insecure about having people stick around."

"Yeah, I guess he is," I agreed. "I hope you told him I wasn't planning to leave him?"

"I told him," she said, and I could breathe again. "Kind of hard to convince him while you're spending the day seeing your new studio though."

"It's not my new studio," I said, feeling suddenly hollow. "I didn't sign yet or anything."

"Do you want to?" she asked.

"Maybe," he admitted. "It is pretty amazing. It's a huge step up from where we are."

"Well, you know I'm down," she said. "I'll move to LA in a heartbeat as long as business expenses are covered."

I chuckled.

"You'll come, perfect... now I need to see about Jaime."

She feigned a dramatic gasp.

"You've only been dating for two weeks and now you want to ask him to move cities with you?" she asked. "Why am I not surprised?"

"What is that supposed to mean?" I asked.

"Just that you two look at each other like there's no one else in the room."

"Jealous?" I asked as my heart swelled.

"Absolutely."

I shook my head.

"Okay, let me call Jaime and see how he is."

"Good luck," she said in parting.

I rang Jaime's number, fingers drumming against the untouched wrapper of the sandwich I'd bought.

When he didn't answer, I forced myself not to worry, to take a time out and eat before trying again.

My neglected coffee was already lukewarm, but the sandwich was good. Still, I tore through it, eager to call Jaime again.

Again, he didn't answer, so I sent a text.

> Are you up to something? I tried calling.

Sorry, I didn't hear it.

I stared at the weak lie. He had texted back straight away, so obviously, he just didn't want to talk. Guessing the reason, I sent another message.

> Today went great. How was the driving lesson?

There was a brief wait this time for a reply.

It was great. Drove around the block.

I stared for a long time, sadness filling me. For a while, I thought about playing along. He obviously was trying to save face, but I didn't want him to be that way with me. He didn't need to pretend to be strong. We were honest with each other. That was something I loved about being with him.

Biting my lip, I decided to come clean.

> Naomi told me what happened.

This time, there was a very long wait for his reply.

I looked out the window at the large, sweeping street packed with all different kinds of people walking by.

Finally, my phone vibrated.

> I didn't want you to worry.

I smiled sadly. This was the type of stuff I wanted him to share with me. But before I could type a reply he wrote another message, changing the topic.

> How was the studio tour?

> Amazing. It really blew me away.

> So, when do you start? Lol

> I haven't signed anything yet, don't worry.

> I'm about to head back to Gaynor. Can I come to your place? Might be there late.

> Yes. Come over.

I smiled.

> Don't wait up for me.

> I wont.

> I can't wait to climb into bed and wrap you up in my arms.

> I miss you too.

Feeling soothed, I stood up, ready to get back to my man as quickly as possible.

It only verified the fact that I would never be able to move to LA without him. Naomi was right though. It was strange of me to think about inviting him when we had been together for such a short amount of time. It seemed like living together properly would be the better next step. Maybe I could commute? Or come back on weekends?

I started to laugh as I made it slowly through the city because it suddenly hit me that we had never even made things official between us. By the time I was pulling onto the number five, I resolved to change that.

I would make it clear how much Jaime meant to me, and if he wasn't into any of the quick ideas I'd formed, we'd come up with a new one together.

CHAPTER 21
JAIME

I T WAS PROBABLY SELFISH TO WANT ETHAN TO GET HOME AS quickly as possible. He'd had a really long day and probably wanted to go home for a change of clothes or something, but I wanted as much time with him as possible before he decided on the inevitable.

At about seven-thirty, I managed to get Evie into her bed, after a bath and a bottle. After that, I sat in front of the TV, watching random cooking shows while I waited for Ethan.

He'd told me to go to bed ahead of him, since he knew I tended to pass out early since Evie interrupted my sleep and sleeping in past five wasn't always a guarantee. I wanted to wait up a bit longer though. I wanted to greet him with a kiss and hear all about his day. Even though I was worried about what it would mean for us, I was still excited for him. To support or encourage him in any way on this journey made me feel like I was helping his legacy. Whenever he spoke about his work, it was with tenderness and love, and the thought of him reaching more people was touching. If anyone deserved it, he did.

But that didn't mean I wouldn't take every moment I could with him until then.

I sighed, silently berating myself for being so selfish but unable to deny it. I wanted Ethan's sole attention on me. Screw Mr. McIntosh.

As though the universe was ready to deliver, a soft knock sounded on my door.

I'd told him I left the door unlocked for him, but maybe he didn't get the message.

Grinning, I jumped to my feet, excitement to see Ethan making my pulse flutter. God, I had it bad.

I eagerly pulled the door open to greet him.

My gaze met someone else's.

For a moment, I was so surprised, that I didn't register much beyond *this isn't Ethan*. It took a moment for the familiar brown eyes and small frame to sink in.

Liz was standing on my doorstep in a thick, fluffy coat with a backpack slung over one shoulder, gripping it like it was everything she owned—which it probably was. She looked even smaller than I remembered—and more run down.

She didn't say hi or smile. She just gave me a sheepish shrug, looking lost.

I wanted to slam the door shut in her face. I wanted to tell her to get lost even though in a way, I was happy to see her alive and looking okay. But Evie was still her daughter and she had a bigger claim to her than I did, and, for that reason, the sight of my big sister sent a spike of panic through my body.

"Aren't you going to invite me in?" she asked. "I was kind of banking on that."

I stared at her for a moment longer before forcing myself to step back, making room for her to enter.

She stepped into my apartment, pausing as soon as she was inside.

I followed her harrowed gaze to the baby bouncer. There were signs of Evie all over the place: her toys, her empty bottle on the table, yet to be washed, one of her blankets folded on the arm of the couch.

"Where is she?" she asked quietly.

"In the bedroom, asleep."

I led her to my room, allowing the light from the hall to light up the room enough to see the crib without disturbing Evie.

Liz stepped up to the crib, her hands gripping the wooden edge so tightly her knuckles turned white. She looked down at her daughter, took one shuddering breath, and started crying.

I watched for a minute, unsure what to do. The way she looked at Evie's form, with pain and longing and despair struck me deeply. I had no idea what to do or how to help. I just felt hurt suddenly, for both of them.

I turned, heading back to the living room, to give Liz a moment alone and took a seat on the couch, letting my head fall into my hands while I tried to process what was happening and what was going to come next.

"She looks so well cared for."

I looked up at Liz's voice, surprised to see her standing in the doorway to the hall, watching me with wide, red eyes.

"Thank you," I whispered.

Her face crumpled again, a fresh wave of tears pouring from her eyes. She came to me, kneeling in front of me and taking my hands. For a minute, we just watched each other. She shook her head wearily.

"Jaime," she whispered softly, "my little brother… you look so tired."

I chuckled.

"Well, to be fair, I've been up since six."

She shook her head.

"It's more than that." She gulped down more tears, forcing them back. "I dropped a baby on you out of the blue."

I smiled, despite myself.

Why was it that her acknowledging the strain she'd put me under helped lessen it?

"It was—*is* a lot," I said. "But I wouldn't trade Evie for anything."

I wanted her to know that. That if she had any inclination whatsoever to leave her with me, I wanted that. What I didn't want to say, not immediately, not unless I had to, was that I would fight to keep her. I didn't want it to come to that though and my heart raced while I waited for her next words.

"Evie," she repeated. "That's so cute."

I smiled softly.

"It hurt too much to say Evelyn every time."

She smiled sadly.

"But it's a beautiful name…"

"I know," I agreed. "Mom must be happy you named your baby after her, wherever she is."

Liz nodded.

"Do you mind if I stay here for a couple days?" she asked. "I'll just take the couch. You won't even know I'm here. And… It'll be nice for us to catch up. We can all spend time together."

"Of course," I found myself saying.

She beamed, standing and going to her backpack to

pull out a bag of toiletries.

I had so many questions. Where had she been? Where would she be staying next? Was she planning on disappearing again?

Was she going to try to take Evie back?

That gnawed at me while I waited for her.

After a moment, I heard the shower start and forced myself up, getting bedding from the closet and setting up the couch with clean sheets and a fresh pillow and blanket for her.

It was a small thing I could do for her, but I didn't feel like she got thought of much in the places she usually slept, shelters and friends' couches, or sometimes hotels… At rehab things had seemed to be pretty good last time she'd called, but that was more like a hospital than a home and—why was I already thinking this was going to be permanent?

I shook the hopeful thought away.

It never was.

Liz showed up for weeks at a time, convinced me I was about to have my sister back, and then vanished in a puff of smoke. That was just how she was. It had been like this for years. This time, though, the stakes were higher.

By the time she was done in the washroom, I felt completely depleted. I waited outside the door until she emerged, looking a bit fresher, wearing my towel robe, which was huge on her small frame.

"Do you need anything else?" I asked.

She shook her head.

"No, I'm okay. I thought we could sit up and chat for a bit though."

"Would you hate me if I blew you off until the morning? I'm exhausted."

She shook her head.

"That's fine, Jaime, go sleep." She gave me a quick hug. "Thank you."

Her quiet whisper didn't sound like it had much to do with giving her a couch to crash on. More like it was a thank you for keeping her baby alive while she was away.

I shut the door to my room and went to look in at Evie. There was a small plug-in night light on the other side of the room. Just enough to make out her form in the middle of the night when I needed to pick her up.

I looked at her for a moment, listening to the even sound of her breathing long enough that my eyes started to droop, and then crawled into bed, burrowing under the covers.

I longed for Ethan's arms around me, holding me tightly.

Shit. *Ethan.*

He would be here any minute now. Actually, he should have been here already.

I crawled back out of bed, rummaging through my pants until I found my phone. I'd forgotten he was coming over the moment Liz showed up.

> Hit heavy traffic. There was an accident.

> Think I'll head to my place so I don't wake you.

He'd messaged over an hour ago. He was probably back in Gaynor now. Maybe even home already.

I wanted him to be here so badly, but I would have to wait for the morning to get a bear hug from Ethan.

The thought of what tomorrow would bring, of having to face Liz and Evie together nearly made me sick.

CHAPTER 22

ETHAN

Jaime hadn't replied to me last night. I was guessing that was because he was asleep already.

Even though it was nice to wake up in my big bed for once, it just felt wrong for Jaime to not be next to me, breathing evenly.

I sighed.

One day apart and I was pining for him.

How did people function with feelings like these? It put a lot of crazy behavior from friends over the years into perspective. It also made me realize that until now, I'd never really been in love.

Excitement bubbled within me and I leaped from the bed, took the fastest shower in my life, and got dressed. Within a few minutes, I was in my car, heading to Ethan's place.

I detoured for coffees and donuts and parked on the street, eager to surprise him.

The door was locked when I tried to open it, so I knocked.

After a moment, I heard footsteps approaching. I

smiled in anticipation.

Jaime answered, looking a little distracted. He was still in his pajamas, his hair not yet brushed and tangled on one side from sleep.

My heart gave a little flip and without even a hello, I dipped down, catching his lips against mine for a brief kiss.

He blinked.

"Oh. Ethan."

I raised a brow. *Oh, Ethan?* If not for the relief in his voice, I would have been offended.

"Were you expecting someone else?" I joked.

He glanced back into the apartment, and then instead of letting me in, stepped out in his bare feet, carefully shutting the door behind himself before stepping eagerly up to me, wrapping his arms around my shoulders and holding on tight.

My hands were full, but I wrapped my arms around him, holding him as my heart raced.

"What happened? Are you okay?"

He nodded with his face still pressed against my neck.

"I'm okay."

"Evie?"

"She's okay."

He drew back enough to meet my gaze. He looked exhausted.

"What is it, Jaime? What happened?"

He forced a small smile.

"Liz is here."

For a moment, I didn't know how to react.

"I thought she was in rehab."

"Last I heard," he agreed. "Looks like she's been out for a couple weeks, couch surfing."

"Oh."

We watched each other for a moment and the silent question grew louder and louder until I had to say it.

"What does this mean?" I asked. "Is she here for Evie?"

He swallowed, brows twitching into a worried frown.

"I'm not sure," he whispered. "She hasn't said and I'm too afraid to ask."

His hands tightened in the fabric of my jacket.

"She only gave me guardianship. I don't really have a claim to her. If she tries to take her..."

He was shaking, top to bottom, and I didn't think it had anything to do with the morning chill, but I squeezed him tightly, pressed a kiss to his cheeks and gently steered him back toward the door.

"Come on, it's cold out here. We'll deal with this however is best for Evie."

He didn't seem very happy with that statement but managed to nod.

Before he could open the door though, I pressed another kiss to his cheek.

"I'll be here to help, Jamie. In any way that I can."

He took a shaky breath, nodded, and then went inside, holding the door open for me.

As soon as I stepped inside, I was met with the sight of Jaime's older sister sitting on the couch with Evie held carefully in her arms. She was a slight woman, small in height and stature, with a pixie face, long brown hair pulled back into a tight ponytail, and huge brown eyes that rose to stare at me while I entered.

"Hi," she said slowly, giving Jaime a look.

"This is Ethan," he said. "My boyfriend."

He didn't look at me when he said it, adding the words so quickly I thought he might be hoping it went unnoticed.

No such luck. Hearing him call me that nearly made me melt into a puddle on the floor and Liz's already big eyes went even bigger.

"Oh. When did *that* happen?" she asked, staring between us.

Jaime shrugged, rubbing a hand through his hair.

"I'll be right back," he muttered and took off for the bathroom, probably to get away for a minute.

I bit my lip, wanting to go after him, but Liz was already talking to me.

"Wow, so you're my brother's man, huh?" she asked.

I resigned myself to sitting and talking. I would just have to grab Jaime and kiss him silly another time.

"Yes, Ethan. Nice to meet you."

I offered her my hand and she shifted Evie around to take it, shaking mine with a strong grip.

"Nice to meet you," she said.

I sank into the spot next to her, reaching out to touch Evie's hand and smiling when she took it, giving me a wide-eyed stare.

"Hello Evie," I said. "Did you miss me?"

When she returned my smile with a happy noise, I laughed.

"How cute is she?"

"Adorable," Liz agreed. "She's grown so much."

The tone of her voice drew my gaze.

She was watching Evie sadly. Her big brown eyes were expressive, just like Jaime's, and it was easy to see the pain there.

"I know you've been through a lot," I found myself saying, "but you did the right thing for her, leaving her with your brother. Jaime would die before he let anything bad happen to her."

She swallowed thickly and forced a nod.

"I didn't know that at the time. I just needed her to go somewhere safe. I didn't know he would do such a good job though... He's always been my bratty little brother, you know?"

She smiled fondly.

"Now, it looks like he's all grown up."

She gave me a look, her eyes mischievous in a way that reminded me a little bit of Naomi when she started needling me about my love life.

"So, how did you two meet?" she asked.

"Jaime brought Evie to one of my readings at the bookstore."

Her brows rose.

"You're a writer?"

"Kids' books," Jaime said from the hallway where he was leaning and watching us interact. "He has a show too."

He met my gaze, his expression filled with warmth. How much of that had he heard?

Liz stared between us. "No way!" she said in awe.

To my chagrin, Jaime excitedly brought out the collection of books I'd given him, and basically began giving her a full run down of my career.

"He just got picked up by a huge network too," Jaime was saying proudly.

They'd set Evie down on her mat and were sitting on the floor now, discussing me like I wasn't here. It was pretty sweet how they interacted: the banter and teasing that only siblings could pull off was clear between them, the love obvious.

"Wow, look at you, dating a real celebrity. So fancy."

"I'm not a celebrity," I sighed for the fourth time, and

they both laughed. "Do you see any paparazzi anywhere?"

Jaime snorted.

"I've seen people ask for your autograph."

"Only at the bookstore," I said, blushing. Then, to change the topic, I remembered the box of donuts I'd bought and handed it to them on the floor.

"Dibs on the chocolate!" Jaime said immediately.

Liz rolled her eyes, chuckling.

"You always say that, and I don't even want the chocolate. I want the sprinkles."

She picked out the one she wanted but instead of taking his, Jaime sat up, lifting the box up for me to pick one first.

"Which one do you want?" he asked.

"I'll take this jelly one," I said, touched.

"You can have the chocolate one," he insisted. "I don't mind."

I shook my head, but before he went back to lying down I couldn't resist dipping in for a kiss.

His thick lashes fluttered shut for a moment, but he didn't lean in for more when I pulled back because his sister was quiet, obviously watching the exchange.

Jaime took his donut, and we all ate in silence.

I wasn't sure what to make of Liz. She wasn't quite like I expected her to be. Based on the little I had heard, I had thought she would be a bit wilder, maybe a bit erratic, and maybe she *could* get that way in her dark times, but right now, she was sharp as a hawk, her gaze shooting around, not missing a detail. All the while, she was hard to read. Apart from fondness for her brother and a bit of a playful nature, I had no clue why she was here. No wonder Jaime was worried.

When Evie suddenly started to cry, Jaime moved automatically, gathering her up and getting a bottle to her in record time.

Liz was watching with those sharp eyes, still sitting back, eating another donut while she did.

We were all quiet and when Evie fell asleep, Jaime stood.

"I'm just going to put her in bed," he said quietly.

We both nodded.

I didn't think much of it until it took too long for Jaime to come back.

I stood, immediately overtaken by worry, and followed him to the bedroom, pausing only when I reached the doorway at the scene within.

Evie was asleep in her crib, but Jaime was sitting on the edge of the bed, looking down at his phone. His shoulders were stooped, his entire body looked dejected, his eyes completely lost.

Quietly, I crept to his side, slowly sinking down next to him. The moment my arm went around his shoulders, he leaned against me, seeking comfort.

"What is it?" I asked.

He handed me his phone. It was open on an email reply from Tiny Tots Daycare. They were full.

I blinked at the reply, reading it twice before speaking.

"That's not so bad, is it?"

He didn't respond for a long minute.

"Without daycare, I can't get my GED or go to school or even get a job."

"They said Evie can be added to the waitlist," I said gently. "I'm sure they'll have room for her soon. Do you want me to respond for you?"

"What's the point?" he asked, his voice suddenly heavy. "She might be gone soon."

I pulled Jaime in to a tight embrace, holding him steady while he tried to breathe.

"You need to talk to her," I whispered. "Whatever her decision, you need to know what it is, to be prepared for it."

He swallowed.

"I'm not ready," he choked.

His whole body was shaking.

I closed my arms around Jaime, holding him tightly to me while he fell apart, tears soaking my shoulder.

From what Jaime had told me, Liz had made this arrangement feel more permanent than this. She had dropped Evie off and been out of touch with a warning that she needed space. He'd thought this was forever; otherwise, he wouldn't call Evie his daughter. For Liz to return so soon... It was messy. That was for sure.

I wished I could help in some way, but all I could do was hold him and wish away the pain.

I stroked Jaime's back, whispering soothing words.

"It's not set in stone yet," I whispered softly. "Just wait and see."

Liz might not even *want* her baby back. I didn't want to sound harsh, but it was what Jaime wanted anyway. She'd left her with him for a reason... yes, that didn't mean it was permanent, but the fact that Jaime seemed convinced that the purpose of her visit was to take Evie back was a bit of a mystery. It could just as easily go the other way.

Jaime shook his head stubbornly, even as tears continued to fall.

"Nothing ever works out for me," he whispered.

That statement was harder to argue with, even if I didn't like it. Did that mean he thought our relationship was temporary too?

CHAPTER 23

JAIME

I COULDN'T HELP THE FEELING OF DREAD IN THE PIT OF MY stomach. For a couple weeks I'd had it all. Evie, Ethan, and hope for the future.

Now Evie was going to be taken away, and I'd lose track of her and Liz, like I always did. Then Ethan would have enough and move on to his big new job, and I would be back at square one, trying to find my footing all over again.

It took all of my strength to pull myself back together again and keep my mouth shut. I didn't want Ethan to feel bad. I wanted the best for him and that meant moving on with his career and life. He didn't need to hold me together forever.

I would figure myself out, somehow. It seemed like an impossible task, but I would manage just like I always had.

For now, I focused on the feeling of his strong hand, stroking my back over the shirt, the feel of his chest rising and falling against mine, the subtle musk of his scent and the scrape of his stubble against my temple.

"God, you're so wonderful," I whispered.

He reached for my chin, tilting my face up to meet his so he could kiss me. I sank even further into his touch, feeling soothed for a moment longer.

How did Ethan always seem to know what I needed?

"I'm all yours, Jaime," he said softly, and my eyes opened, meeting his crisp blue gaze, filled with empathy and what I hoped was love.

"You don't need to say that," I whispered. "About the boyfriend thing, I didn't want to introduce you as *just* my friend, but you don't need to feel pressured—"

"That's not it," he said firmly. "I want it to be official, because I'm not going anywhere."

He took my face in his hands and looked directly into me.

"Jaime, I love you."

My heart tripped at his words. It took a moment to steady myself.

"Ethan…"

Suddenly my heart was racing, blood ringing in my ears, hope shooting through me like electricity.

"Don't say that," I replied shakily.

"It's the truth," he whispered.

I pressed forward, sealing our lips together desperately.

"I—I—"

"You don't have to say anything," he said gently. "I just want you to know."

I *wanted* to say it though, because it was the truth. I loved him. I loved him so much that it was overwhelming, but I was scared to say it. If I put it out there, if he knew, it would make everything harder.

Instead, I pressed our lips together again, sinking into his embrace, letting him take charge the way that he did. The way that made all the worries pour out of me, leaving me boneless and relaxed.

When he pulled back, I didn't want to let him go. But he was right to, of course, because I heard the washroom door close quietly. The bedroom door was open, the bathroom door was visible from where we sat. I'd almost forgotten that Liz was here. Ethan's mouth had that effect on me.

In strong hands, he took my cheeks, holding me there until he had my undivided attention.

"Everything is going to be okay," he said firmly. "Trust me."

For some reason, I did.

I let Ethan hold me for a while longer. When Liz emerged from the washroom, she didn't glance in at us on her way back to the living room.

This whole situation felt weird and uncomfortable. I wanted Liz in my life, but I was afraid of her being there.

But Ethan offered me a strength I didn't know I could have again so easily. With his hand in mine, I felt like I could breathe again, at least long enough to find out what would come next. I could face it so long as I wasn't alone.

As for his job, I'd been too chicken to even ask about it yet, so I would just have to wait for him to tell me. And based on the way he was being with me, wanting to be my boyfriend and all, I would just have to trust he would try to make it work for both of us.

A touch of skepticism rose within me, but I pushed it back down.

If he wanted to try to make this work long-term, I was

curious to see what he came up with. If it was doable at all, I would be in one hundred and ten percent.

For now, as he said, I just had to trust.

CHAPTER 24

ETHAN

Liz was surprisingly cheerful for the day. She didn't seem to mind spending time around us, the couple that couldn't stop gazing at each other or touching with a hand on an arm or knee or a quick embrace or even occasional kisses when we didn't think she was looking.

She caught us more than once, but she only smiled lightly.

She didn't pay us too much attention at all, really, she was too focused on Evie. She insisted on taking over feeding her and when we all went out for a walk, she wore the carrier instead of Jaime.

I could see the corners of his eyes crease with worry, but he kept it to himself, keeping the conversation light, even when his grip tightened on my hand.

When Evie started wailing for a few minutes, and no amount of Liz's bouncing stopped her, was the only time he intervened.

"I'll take her," he insisted, reaching for her, but Liz shook her head, frowning and turning her back to us as she walked away, still bouncing Evie.

Jaime bit his lip, watching anxiously. I tugged him toward a park bench, forcing him to sit down at least so he wouldn't start pacing.

He started to bite a nail at once, his gaze still glued to them.

"You have more experience than Liz does," I reminded him. "It'll take some time for her to get the hang of baby language."

His frown deepened.

"So you *do* think she's going to take Evie."

"I didn't say that, but it does look like she wants to be involved with her somehow, doesn't it?"

He sagged, nodding.

"That wouldn't necessarily be a bad thing, would it?" I asked. "For Evie to know her mother?"

He swallowed but finally shook his head.

"No, it would be good," he finally said. "I can't help feeling threatened though."

"I can't imagine how hard this is."

That finally drew his gaze, some softness entering it.

"You're making it a little bit easier for me," he said. "Thank you."

Before I could respond, Liz marched back, grinning triumphantly. Evie was quiet, looking around with her trademark wide eyes. Suddenly, I realized how like Liz's they were. Big and round with pale, straight brows. The color was the only difference.

"I did it! Look, she's quieted down."

Jaime smiled, real warmth seeping into the expression.

"That's good, Liz! She'll be used to you in no time," he said standing.

I was surprised but pleased to see that, in the end, Jaime was most concerned with everyone winning out. He just seemed to think that, no matter what, it came at *his* expense.

When we got back home, Liz insisted on making dinner, and I finally noticed that I'd been accosted with ignored phone calls and messages. Mostly from Naomi and Arty but a couple from my dad too. Everyone was dying to know how the studio tour had gone. At seeing the indignant angry face emoji from Naomi after being ignored all day, I finally relented.

"I'm just going to make a couple calls," I told Jaime.

He nodded and I went outside, taking a seat in the rickety garden chair nearby before dialing.

"I'm alive," I said at once.

"And?" she demanded, "what did Jaime say? Did you ask him to come with you?"

"No, no. Not yet... maybe not at all."

There was a long silence.

"What? I thought you were dead set on being with Jaime."

"I am. I'm just not dead set on the studio."

"Because of him?"

I shrugged even though she couldn't see me.

"I don't want to rock the boat right now. He's already going through a lot."

"Okay," she said slowly. "You might not want to put it that way for Arty. He's so excited."

I could practically hear her grimace.

"Yeah, I know. I'll just tell him I need some more time to decide. I'll make up a reason."

She chuckled softly.

"I can't believe you went from blowing off guys for work to blowing off work for a guy. Never thought I'd see the day."

I found myself smiling softly.

"Yeah, well, Jaime's not just any guy. He's special."

"Awww."

She made a soft, gushy sort of sound, the same one I'd heard her do whenever the little kids did something cute.

"That's my cue," I chuckled. "I have to call Arty and my dad to give them updates."

"Alright, good luck."

Arty was buzzed. He'd seen the studio before they'd suggested the arrangement to me, and he had been on the edge of his seat waiting for my approval. Telling him how excited it made me feel and how nice I thought it was helped ease into the fact that I wasn't dead set on it yet. My excuse of not being ready to leave my hometown seemed to help ease him off a bit.

Then there was my dad.

The deep, familiar sound of his voice soothed me like nothing else. Until finding Jaime, I'd never thought I would find another person who I would love like family. Now, suddenly, I had both him and Evie and life felt different from top to bottom.

"Hey, Buddy, I was waiting for your call."

"I know, sorry, Dad."

"How was the city?"

"Alright," I answered.

The fact that that was his first question, that I had told him about work, but not about Jaime, bothered me.

"You know, it was okay, but it made me realize a couple things..."

"Oh yeah?" he asked.

My dad was great that way, ever patient and calm no matter what. I often thought that nothing could shock him more than the things that had already happened in his life.

"Now that I've gone to see it, I find I'm more interested in making sure things still work with this guy I've been seeing."

He was quiet for a moment.

"What's his name?"

"Jaime," I said and then everything started tumbling out. "And he has a little girl—his niece actually, but he cares for her. He's been a bit down on his luck for a while but since we met there's this connection between us..."

I swallowed, unsure why I was sharing all of this now. Maybe for his advice on how to move forward.

"What kind of connection?" he asked. "Physical?"

"I mean, yeah, that's definitely there, but there's more than that. Something solid, like we can rely on each other too." I leaned back, trying to put words to the way it felt when we were together. "It's like we fill in each other's cracks... I don't know."

I chuckled, feeling foolish, but my dad was silent for a long minute.

"Ethan, if you found something like that, then that's the number one thing you should be prioritizing," he said. His voice was full of emotion and it hit me, making my heart hurt and eyes sting. "When you're on your deathbed, you won't be thinking about how much money you made. You'll be thinking about the people you care about and if you did enough for them, if you got enough moments with them. I know I'll be thinking about you, your mom and sister, even after all this time. I don't want you to have any of those big regrets, son, like I do."

I blinked back tears, forcing air into my lungs.

"Yeah," I agreed. "I know you're right. It's not a long commute, but being gone five days a week, probably ten-plus hours wouldn't work for us. Moving makes more sense, but I don't know if I want to leave the life I've built here. I like the little things, like reading at the library and even our small studio."

"Of course," he enthused, "because you did it all yourself. You built up your career, following your heart every step of the way. Ethan, you've been an inspiration."

"Thanks, Dad," I managed.

"I don't see why you have to do it at all," he mused. "You've done everything your way thus far and it's worked, right? If you want to grow the show, why not do it how *you* want to?"

"Hm. I hadn't thought of that."

He chuckled, a deep burly sound that filled me with nostalgia.

"That's why you called your old man," he said proudly.

I chuckled.

"I guess so. You've given me a lot to think about."

Maybe it was time to completely rearrange my life, the way that *I* would want it. I'd been content enough before, but now it seemed like it was time for change. I couldn't turn down the LA offer without a backup plan, one that would suit me and Jaime and, hopefully, Evie too if Liz was okay with that.

"I should head back in," I said. "I'm at Jaime's place now."

"I'm looking forward to meeting him," my dad said warmly. "Any man good enough for my son must be special."

I smiled.

"Thanks, Dad," I said, "for everything... hopefully I'll be able to be as good a parent as you are."

"Alright, that's enough making me tear up for one day," he said gruffly. "Off you go."

I chuckled and hung up, my mind reeling.

When I thought of Jaime, I had complete confidence in *us*. But he didn't want to hold me back, that much was clear. Part of me knew he loved me, but he was too afraid to say it back. That didn't bother me. Ever since the start, Jaime had needed me to take the lead and I loved giving him what he needed.

Somehow, I would have to convince him that staying here with him was worthwhile for me. But not yet. Once we knew Liz's plans, I would go from there. Either way, I would be there for him on every step of this journey.

CHAPTER 25

JAIME

ME AND LIZ WERE DISCUSSING DINNER BY THE TIME ETHAN re-entered. He came straight to where I was sitting on the floor and spread out next to me, his back against the couch so we were side by side, his long legs stretched out beside mine.

Sitting on the armchair playing with Evie, Liz gave me a look that made me shrug, my cheeks heating.

"You two are so damn cute!" she said, unable to keep it to herself. "The way that you look at each other!"

She pretended to fan herself.

I groaned, but Ethan just smiled, looking at me exactly the way she was talking about.

Dammit, I couldn't wait to be alone with him. A couple of days without being able to really snuggle against him sucked. I wanted him without the clothes on too, his hard cock turning me into a puddle on the bed, making me completely fall apart and forget everything but the all-too-good feeling of him inside me.

I forced my gaze back to Evie and Liz, reminding my touch-deprived cock that this wasn't the time to get hard.

"So, dinner," I said loudly, forcing the conversation back. "I can always cook something instead of ordering."

"Like what?" she asked.

"Pasta, a chicken stir-fry..." I tried to remember what I had in the fridge. "Mashed potatoes and sausages?"

Her eyes widened hopefully.

"You make the best mashed potatoes."

"Does he?" Ethan asked.

She nodded.

"Any roast-type stuff. Scalloped potatoes, cauliflower cheese... he makes a great turkey too."

I shrugged self-consciously at the impressed look Ethan was giving me.

"I like to cook," I muttered.

"You've been holding out on me. I can't wait to try."

I pushed myself up, grinning.

"I'll get everything started."

Cooking always felt like a timeout for me, my thoughts turned from everything else to focus on the task at hand, the flavors and textures. In that sense, it was like sex, a solid, almost meditative distraction.

I could hear them chatting in the living room, getting to know each other while I started cooking. For a while, everything felt sort of peaceful and domestic. Then Ethan came in and wrapped his arms around my waist from behind, pressing a kiss to my neck and it was even better.

I sighed, leaning back against him, soaking in the feeling of being in his arms and the momentary tranquility.

It was broken, almost at once, by a loud wail from the living room.

As one, both Ethan and I stilled, listening as Evie screamed.

Instinctively, I thought it sounded like she wanted her bottle. If not for the fact that Liz had been adamant to not let me take her this afternoon, I would already be there, feeding her.

Instead, despite how much it hurt, I remained where I was, waiting to see what Liz would do.

To my immense relief, after a minute, I heard her approach.

She paused in the doorway, looking worn and agitated, baleful eyes on me and Ethan.

"I don't know what she wants," she said.

Ethan moved for me, releasing me and going to them, gently taking Evie from her.

"I'll give you both a break," he said, smiling warmly at her like she'd done nothing wrong. She hadn't, but I knew how comforting that look was when Ethan stepped in like that. With one soft smile, he was able to tell you everything was fine and Liz... burst into tears.

Shocked, for a moment, we both stood still, staring as sobs began to wrack her small body.

Finally, I moved to her, taking her narrow shoulders in my hands.

"Liz, what is it?" I asked, although I could guess. This couldn't be easy for her.

For a moment, she choked on an answer but couldn't get any words out.

I pulled her into a quick hug, holding her while my heart pounded. I couldn't imagine what she was going through, not knowing her own daughter.

"Come here," I muttered, steering her toward the table.

She collapsed into the chair, grabbing anv piece of paper towel to dry her face while she did.

Ethan sank into the chair opposite her, finally quieting Evie with a bottle.

"I'm such shit at this," she finally gasped.

Instinctively, I started to argue, but she shook her head frantically, bits of hair flying free around her face.

"No, I am. I knew I would be. I can't be a mom."

I wasn't sure how to react. In the face of Liz's tears, it felt dirty to be happy about what she was saying. I couldn't be.

My eyes flew to Ethan's. He met my gaze, his filled with compassion.

"You just need some experience," I found myself saying, echoing Ethan's earlier sentiment. "It takes practice to read a baby. I've known Evie longer. I spent every moment with her all this time."

"It's not just that," she sniffled.

It took her another minute of wiping tears before she could go on.

"I'm not fit for this yet. I don't even have anywhere to live yet. Even if I did..." She took a shuddering breath. "No, I knew when I gave her to you it was probably going to be permanent, I just didn't want to admit it at the time."

She looked up at me, tears still streaming from her red eyes.

"Please don't hate me for this, but seeing her with you two..." She swallowed and pressed on. "I don't think Evelyn was ever supposed to be mine. I think I had her for you."

"Liz," I choked.

"With you, she has a real family. I don't know if I'll ever be able to give her that. It'll take a few years, I'm thinking, before I can be stable enough for a family and it wouldn't be fair to take her away from you after all that time."

My eyes stung with tears. I tried to blink them back but couldn't.

They poured free as I sank down in front of her chair, taking her trumping hands in my own.

"Liz," I said gently, "I'm so sorry."

A fresh wave of tears poured from her eyes.

"I should be apologizing to *you*. You didn't ask for this."

"Maybe," I admitted, "but I want it. I would be heart-broken if you took her."

Finally telling Liz that lifted a weight from my shoulders and the way she lit up a little bit helped.

"Do you mean that?" she asked. "I can't tell you how guilty I've felt."

"It was a lot at first," I admitted. "But I would be devastated without her."

"I don't think Evie is too unhappy with the arrangement either," Ethan added. "She's a very happy, healthy baby."

She looked between us three, smiling sadly.

"I hope you won't mind if I'm still around, will you? I'd still like to know her and maybe even be involved sometimes, if it's not too much."

I shook my head fervently.

"No, Liz, I *want* you around. I miss you."

The tears started again, for both of us. We ended up hugging and crying while Ethan sat feeding Evie across the table, watching with warm, sad eyes.

Only the sound of the water overflowing and hitting the hob finally drew us apart.

"Shit, the potatoes," I muttered, and for some reason, that made us all laugh.

The rest of the night passed in a haze.

Ethan was unnecessarily impressed by the roast dinner I threw together. Evie was in a happy mood, smiling at anyone who looked at her, and me and Liz kept smiling too, when tears didn't burn our eyes.

I was overwhelmed. I should have been used to the feeling, but I wasn't. Aside from the first while with Ethan, I hadn't ever felt this *good* kind of overwhelmed. The kind where everything seemed to be working out and you were so grateful and so scared that you didn't know how to process.

For a while, I'd ridden the buzz, planning my future with Ethan until he got news of his promotion and I hadn't been able to drive and Liz had shown up and basically, nothing had worked out for me.

Did that mean more would come crashing down around me as soon as I let my guard drop?

For some reason, I didn't think so.

This felt different.

It felt like I had made it through the deep end and I didn't have to hold my breath any longer.

Yes, Ethan's job was still up in the air, but when I met his gaze and felt the strength of feelings between us, instead of fearing losing him, I felt hope.

CHAPTER 26

ETHAN

JAIME LOOKED DEVASTATED WHEN WE ENTERED THE LIVING room early in the morning to find Liz already clean and dressed, with makeup on, putting her earrings in.

Her bedding was folded neatly and sitting on the coffee table, her bag packed.

"What are you doing?" he demanded.

"Getting out of your hair," she said, smiling. "I want to get out of the way. This place isn't big enough for all four of us."

"It is!" Jaime argued, but she stood up and gave him a hug.

"I'll still be nearby. I'm going to stay with Doug for a bit."

"Doug?" Jaime repeated numbly.

She gave him a shrewd smile.

"Don't worry, he told me he's sober now."

For both Jaime and Liz's sake, I hoped that was true.

"I don't stay here all the time," I said, wondering if that would sway her, but she shook her head.

"Honestly... it's too hard for me right now. I'm happy

for how everything has worked out, but it still makes me feel like shit."

She shrugged helplessly.

"Baby steps, I think. If I see Evie for a little while every couple of days, I'll probably get used to this, but for now, I need some space and you two lovebirds do too."

She winked, lifting her backpack onto her shoulders.

"I'll call you, okay?"

"Yeah, alright," Jaime said dejectedly. "Just promise, if he's not actually sober, you'll come back here?"

She paused.

"We can stay at Ethan's and you can have the whole place to yourself."

He glanced at me, making sure I didn't mind.

I nodded, letting my arm rest around his shoulders.

She chuckled.

"Fine, fine. I promise."

Evie let out a cry and Jaime sighed heavily.

"I'll call you," he promised and slid out from my half embrace to go attend to his daughter.

"See you," Liz said, smiling, but when she reached for the door handle, she paused, her head bowed.

"What is it?" I asked.

Liz took a slow breath and turned back around to face me.

"You seem like a nice guy," she said sincerely. "But Jaime's had enough people let him down. Don't be one of them."

With that, she turned and left.

I stood there for a moment, still staring at the closed door.

I had no intention of letting Jaime down or hurting him

in any way, but her words sparked something in me. An idea.

His distrust in this working out came from his past. She was right. Everyone he had loved had let him down—even Liz did it repeatedly.

To give Jaime true confidence in *us*, maybe I needed to go the extra mile.

CHAPTER 27

JAIME

> There's an UBER outside waiting for you.

I PAUSED, READING THE MESSAGE A SECOND TIME BEFORE MY gaze flew to the window to see a white Tesla parked with a big UBER sticker on the front.

"What the hell?" I muttered.

Ethan had gone to work in the morning, then insisted on sending Naomi to my place in the afternoon so that I could get out of the house for a bit.

I'd been whining about needing some time to get some stuff done, so had taken the opportunity to go to the cafe and work on my laptop. Now that I'd been here for two hours fiddling with a resume that I probably couldn't use and browsing jobs that I couldn't apply for, I was glad for the distraction.

I stood up, quickly packing my things and tossing what was left of my coffee.

What was Ethan planning?

We hadn't been able to have another date since that first one.

Grinning, I climbed into the cab.

"Hi," I said.

"Hello," the driver said, smiling. "Jaime?"

"Yes."

I tapped a foot as he pulled out, but I couldn't resist asking.

"Where are we going?"

He raised a brow, then looked at his directions.

"Uh, it looks like we're headed to Gaynor Heights. Is that right?"

I nodded, heart starting to race with anticipation.

Ethan, that sneaky bastard had sent his assistant to babysit, then got me a cab to his place. No one but us. No distractions.

I was practically melting and I wasn't even there yet. I'd never had anyone do something so romantic.

My stomach was a flutter of nerves by the time we arrived at his place.

I thanked the driver and practically ran for the front door.

Ethan was waiting for me because he opened it before I could knock, meeting me as I threw myself into his arms.

He laughed, holding me to his chest for a long minute.

"What is this?" I asked, grinning. "Sneaking me out for a date?"

I pulled back far enough that I could kiss him.

His hands slid into my hair, tilting my head to deepen the kiss until I was a wreck, hard and loose as putty in his arms.

With a groan, he pulled back.

"Wait, not too eager now, we have to speak first."

That ominous line had me straightening at once,

pulling back to look at him properly without excitement blinding me.

"Shit," I muttered at his obviously nervous expression.

"No," he murmured, kissing me again. "It's nothing bad. I hope."

"Then why did you have to bring me here to talk about it?" I asked, extracting myself from his arms.

Now my heart was racing for a different reason.

He wasn't acting like he was about to dump me; he'd said not *yet* to the kissing, after all.

"Is this about that job?" I asked, swallowing. "You're right, it's probably time to rip off the bandage... I've already prepared myself for anything you might say."

I tilted my chin, waiting and pretending I was ready to hear about doing this long distance. That seemed like the most obvious solution, and I appreciated that he was probably still going to try to be with me for a while.

Ethan frowned, and stepped up to me, wrapping me in his embrace again.

"Can you please not jump to conclusions?" he asked gently. "I do need to talk to you about that, but there's something else I want to talk about first."

His heart thudded against mine and my nerves spiked higher.

"What is it?" I asked nervously.

He swallowed.

"I want to show you something... Oh god, I really hope you don't hate me for this."

My eyes widened.

"Ethan, what the hell? Please stop dragging this on. I'm dying here."

He snorted and released me, but he took my hand.

"Now, this doesn't need to be permanent if you don't

like it," he said as he led me up the stairs. "I know it might be a lot."

He stroked my knuckles with his thumb as we walked down the hall to one of the spare bedrooms. At the door, Ethan paused and turned to look at me.

"I don't want you to feel pressured into this, it can all be undone, but if you want it as much as I do, just know, you and Evie are the most important parts of my life now and I want to make sure it stays that way."

With that, he pushed the door open, revealing a nursery.

For a moment, I couldn't breathe.

I walked into the room, turning in a slow circle to take it all in. The walls were painted a soft gray with puffy clouds floating by. Floating shelves held familiar toys and story books. A comfortable looking rocking chair was set next to the crib. All around soft decorations, pillows and baby blankets and rugs with cute designs livened the place up.

"This is her crib," I whispered, "and her blankets..."

"And most of her toys," Ethan added, still sounding nervous.

I turned to look at him, my eyes wide.

"Ethan, when did you have time to do this?" I demanded.

He shrugged sheepishly. "I painted the walls on Monday, got that rug and those pictures delivered yesterday. Then, today, while you were out, I stopped by your place and picked up the crib and the rest that I could fit in my car."

"How did you have the time?!"

He chuckled.

"I barely did. I had to take the crib apart *and* put it back together."

He stepped up to me, taking my hand again, gaze raking my eyes.

"Does this mean you don't hate this idea?"

"Which idea exactly?" I asked, wanting him to say it.

He smiled gently.

"I want you and Evie to come live with me here."

"Because—"

"Because I love you and don't want to let you go, ever. Whether you like it or not, you two are my family now and I'm not going anywhere."

If I'd wanted proof, this was it. I couldn't argue even if I wanted to, and I didn't. Being here, starting a proper home and family with Ethan, was a dream come true.

I found myself nodding, choking back tears as I threw myself into his arms, embracing him tightly, feeling the relief that flooded his body in the way he started to laugh.

"Oh thank god!" He laughed, squeezing me so hard that I could barely breathe. I laughed in return, holding him just as tightly.

"So, I'm moving in?" I asked, still not believing it.

"Yes," he grinned.

"Now?"

"Whenever you're ready."

"Now."

"Okay," he laughed. "That would be amazing."

He pulled back, kissing me feverishly and I kissed him back, just as excited until he pulled back.

"Not in the nursery, in our room."

"We have a room!" I gushed. "And Evie has her own one."

He laughed, pushing me through the primary bedroom door and shutting it behind us.

"Clothes off," he said, and I couldn't get undressed fast enough.

I climbed into bed while Ethan pulled his shirt over his head. He didn't get far with his pants though, because when he saw me spread out on his sheets, he groaned and dove for me. He gripped my thighs, holding them apart, and buried his face into the crook, licking the seam where my thigh began. Avoiding my cock, he sucked my balls next, pulling one into his mouth and then the other while I bucked.

"Fuck," I groaned, barely getting used to the sensation as he moved lower, licking my hole with a strong swipe of his tongue.

I cried out, arching away from him. He pulled me back down, proceeding to bury his tongue so deep inside me that I was squirming and writing by the time he finally got up to kick his pants free in frustration.

"I'm going to fuck you so hard you see stars," he growled.

I nodded eagerly.

"Please," I whispered.

We hadn't had the chance to do it again, and I was aching for it.

I gripped my knees, pulling them toward my armpits, desperate for it.

Ethan made a guttural noise, watching the display and my hole clenched in anticipation.

He kneeled over me on the bed, slathering his thick cock with lube and then using what remained on his hand to stroke my hole, shutting his eyes in appreciation at the way it opened and closed for him.

Finally, he moved his hand, gripping the insides of both of my knees instead as he positioned himself and slowly pressed inside.

It stung a little, just like last time, but this time, I knew what that minor pain would come with and I didn't care.

His cock stretched me rubbing against my prostate as he pressed in deep. My lips parted, eyes rolling at the sudden intensity of the sensation.

"Like that, baby?"

I nodded, moaning as he did it again.

Ethan took his time with me, like every time, completely wearing me out, slowing or pulling out whenever I was too close.

"Not yet," he grunted each time before starting again, completely undoing me until I was a mess, crying out without control, cock leaking, body weak.

Finally, he pressed his lips to my ear, sucking the lobe and whispering.

"Come for me, sweetheart. Let me see you."

He thrust his cock in deep while he said it, grinding hard at the right angle.

My entire body convulsed with pleasure. Irrepressible tremors ran through me, and I gasped, coming between us without the help of a hand or anything.

Ethan moaned encouragements, stroking my hair, hips flexing against my hole, continuing to grind until he lost control just as completely, groaning and gasping, his cock flexing over and over inside me as he emptied, filling me with delicious heat.

I collapsed like that, satisfied from the tips of my hairs to the bottoms of my feet.

When I woke up, Ethan was dozing next to me, his arms wrapped loosely around me, his light hair sticking up at odd angles. Nothing like the neat Mr. McIntosh he played on TV. It was hard to imagine *that* man commanding with his partners and satisfied in bed.

I stroked my hands gently over the hair on his chest, feeling his masculine body. Everything about Ethan filled me with comfort. I didn't know what it was, just that his presence, the feel of his skin, his breath on my neck—it all filled me with peace.

And I would have this forever.

"What are you thinking about?"

I glanced at Ethan's face, finding him watching me sleepily.

"Just that I get to have this more now, I guess."

He smiled warmly and I wiggled closer, into his arms.

We kissed languidly. No reason to rush.

"This can't be right," I murmured happily. "I can't get *everything*. No one does."

"Maybe you've already paid your dues," he suggested. "Maybe now it's time to enjoy life."

"I like that idea," I said thoughtfully. "But what about your show?"

Leave it to me to ruin a good moment, but suddenly I couldn't resist asking.

""'m not taking it," he said.

I tried to sit up, but Ethan tugged me back down.

"Ethan, you have to. It's such a good opportunity."

"Maybe," he shrugged. "But it's not what I want. Going to talk to everyone this weekend, but I don't want to leave Gaynor or my family. I don't want to commute either. If they want my show, they can take it as is. It doesn't need to be spruced up and made fancy. I like it how it is. And I like having the time to write too. My books are just as important to me."

I lay there for a minute, thoughts racing.

"I suppose you could even start a YouTube channel or something. You could reach loads of people that way. Go beyond this area but still film it here and still be in control."

He froze, and I could see the cogs working in his head.

"Now why didn't I think of that?" he mused.

I chuckled.

"Too old?"

He smacked my ass playfully.

"Watch it," he warned, "or I'll have to punish you."

I grinned, wiggling back to press my ass against his soft cock. It twitched with interest.

"Oh no, please don't," I joked.

Ethan laughed, flipping me and pressing me down into the cushions for another deep kiss.

It didn't linger though, not as much as I wanted it to.

"We should probably go back to your place to get Evie," he said regretfully. "But don't worry, we'll have plenty of time later. We have our own room now after all."

I grinned and shook my head.

"I still can't believe it."

Part of me still felt weird that things were working out like this. I almost wanted to fight it, to protect myself from future heartbreak, but I liked Ethan's way of looking at it better. Why not take it in stride and enjoy the good times? That was what we deserved. And Evie deserved a dad who was willing to give her the best, no matter how scared he was.

My eyes widened.

"I have to call Liz."

I cleaned up in a rush, quickly pulling my boxers and pants back up and fishing out my phone.

"I paid for that place for the year," I explained at Ethan's quizzical look.

His brows shot up.

"Good thinking!"

I bit my lip, excitement blossoming in me.

It was rare for things to just fall into line like this. Maybe that meant it was meant to be.

CHAPTER 28

ETHAN

THE WEEK JAIME MOVED IN HAD BEEN A HAPPY WHIRLWIND. The house had been filled with bags of his belongings, we'd ordered takeout while organizing, and we watched countless movies. It was like fresh life was breathed into the place.

And now, I couldn't imagine my home without my two loves filling the space.

In the month that had passed, Jaime had already started his GED courses and Evie was already sitting up and interacting even more and I couldn't help doting on her.

She still reminded me of Amelia, but that felt like a good thing now. Remembering her—the short time I'd known her—felt distant and special. For a while, I'd had a little sister and now I got to spoil another baby that was just like her. That felt like kismet and the fact that I *could* feel that way was unexpected and special in itself.

I glanced in the rearview mirror and found Evie watching me with her big eyes in her rear facing seat's mirror.

I smiled.

"Hello honey," I said, "you watching me drive?"

She giggled and I took that as a yes as Jaime swiveled in his seat to look at her.

"Aw," he cooed. "She's so damn cute."

"I know, and is it just me or does she keep getting cuter?"

"She does!" Jaime enthused. "How is that possible?"

"I don't know!" I laughed.

I pulled my car to a stop in front of his old place. The sun was shining, so of course, the retired couple, Mr. and Mrs. Woo were outside. Mr. Woo was in the garden, his wife sipping tea and reading a book on the porch.

She stood up as soon as our car pulled up.

Jaime shook his head at me, smiling as he climbed out of the car to talk to them while I took Evie out.

"Hi Jaime!" Mrs Woo was saying. "Can I give you that stuff I told you about?"

Apparently, she had been trying to get Jaime to come to collect some baby items that her grandchildren had grown out of.

Jaime had seemed to be in shock at the time, but we were both surprised when she and her husband went inside, emerging a minute later with a big bag of toys and a baby play center.

"Our granddaughter loved this," she said. "Evie can sit now, right?"

At our nod, she shook her head.

"They grow so fast. Look, you put her legs here and she can feel like she's standing. It will help her build muscles too. And she can play at the same time."

Jaime was in awe, pressing the buttons and seeing

what noises they made. Evie was blown away, reaching for the colorful contraption.

"Why don't we take this inside?" I suggested.

Jaime nodded, smiling from ear to ear.

"Thank you so much," he said warmly, "for everything. I really appreciate it."

They both waved him off.

"We just wanted to help," Mr. Woo said.

Jaime nodded, a frown clouding his smile.

"I can see that now," he said. "I'll still be around a lot with Liz staying here."

"Okay, tell me next time you're coming. I'll make tea."

"I will," he promised.

We put the bag into the car, but Jaime lifted the play center and we walked around to the back. It was weird in the best way to come here from our home to visit someone else.

Liz had been delighted by the arrangement. She didn't need to rely on people's couches while she figured her life out and the freedom had lifted her spirits considerably.

At Jaime's knock, she opened the door, immediately ignoring us to gush over the cute lamb onesie Evie was dressed in. I'd seen it in a shop window and hadn't been able to resist it.

I handed her over, laughing at the way Evie started to giggle.

"Come in!" she said over her shoulder, but Jaime stood in the way for a moment, looking in at the apartment.

After a month of living together in our house, it did look dark and small.

But it had been good for him at the time and now it was good for Liz until she decided otherwise.

"What are you thinking?" I asked.

Jaime looked over his shoulder, meeting my gaze.

"It feels like I was seeing everything *wrong*," he said. "I thought Mr. And Mrs. Woo were judging me, when really they just wanted to help and give me stuff for Evie. I thought Liz being here would mean losing my daughter and that couldn't be further from the truth. I thought being with you could only be temporary and now we're living together. Now everything looks a lot different."

"What's changed?" I asked gently.

"You," he said softly. "You know I love you, right?"

I knew, but that didn't mean my heart didn't swell at his words.

"Put that damn thing down so I can hug you," I whispered.

Jaime chuckled and quickly placed the play center inside the door.

He turned toward me and we wrapped our arms around each other. I didn't ever want to let go. Luckily for us, I knew we would have as much time and as many hugs as we ever needed.

We were in this for life.

EPILOGUE

JAIME

Magda went through the whole spiel again, telling me the basics, just like she did every time.

This was my third try. The first one had been a disaster, but the second one *hadn't* ended in a panic attack, so I took that as a win. I hadn't driven at all, but I had turned on the car with my foot firmly pressing down the brake and that was something.

"Want to try again?" she asked in her usual friendly manner.

I managed to nod, placing my hands on the wheel and glancing back, catching Ethan's gaze in the mirror.

"You've got this," he said at once. "You don't need to drive. Just turn the car on and off."

"It might help if you really feel the brake again too. Feel how well it works."

I nodded, taking calming breaths while I pushed myself to move.

I turned the car on. It didn't move.

I pressed down on the brake, and then, somehow, reached for the gears.

"Good," Magda said softly. "Keep your foot on the brake. Put the car on drive and see how you feel."

Somehow, I did it. The car didn't move at all. Confidence boosted me, even though my heart was racing and my hands were shaking.

"Now, if you lift your foot a bit, you'll see we'll barely move."

It took real strength to go that far, but I pushed myself to try.

The car slid slowly forward and I immediately stomped on the brake pedal too hard, whipping us forward.

"Sorry," I muttered and tried again.

This time, I allowed the car to move about five feet before slowly pressing the brakes back down.

I pulled the emergency brake back up and released everything, my entire body shaking with nerves.

"Can we stop now?" I asked, embarrassed to find that even my voice was trembling.

"Yes, that was great progress," Magda said, patting me.

I agreed.

At this point, countless people had told me I didn't need to do this, but I couldn't help feeling like it was my last hurdle. It was the last thing from my past that was holding me back. For myself, I needed to know that, if necessary, I could get behind the wheel.

"Great job," Ethan said as soon as we got out. "Soon you'll be driving Evie to daycare."

I nodded shakily, even though the idea of that felt miles away.

For the last few weeks, I would take Evie by bus in the mornings and Ethan would pick her up in the afternoon. I was finally starting to get used to us being apart for a few of hours at a time but dropping her off still sucked and I was sure driving wouldn't change that.

I leaned into him, letting him hold me while I breathed.

"I think I need a drink," I sighed.

"Yeah? And dinner, and a movie, and sex?"

"Yes, yes, and yes," I chuckled. "But Naomi…"

I glanced toward the house, finding her in the window with Evie, watching us. She smiled, holding Evie's wrist to make her wave at us.

"We can ask," he said, shrugging. "She usually just watches movies when we're out."

"We should probably find a real babysitter soon," I mused.

"Maybe," Ethan shrugged. "But I pay her well and she's a friend."

Getting Naomi's attention again, he pointed exaggeratedly at me, then himself, then motioned to his car, then pretended to eat.

She laughed, then rolled her eyes and waved us off.

"There you go," Ethan grinned. "She said yes."

I laughed.

"How is everything so easy for you?"

He pulled me toward the car smiling.

"I don't know, but I appreciate it. Every day."

Sitting in the driver's seat, he took my hand in his. Our gazes met.

"Thank you for going on this journey with me, for not pushing me away. I've never been so happy."

I squeezed his hand.

"I feel the exact same way."

END

NEXT IN THE GAYNOR BEACH SERIES

NATE BY AMELIA HAYDEN

Growing up in the foster care system is any kids worst nightmare. Especially so for Nate, who didn't tick any of the traditional boxes. That all changed for him the day he met Ms. Leta. She let him be who he was without judgement. Now, following in her footsteps, Nate has his own brood of foster children with their own complicated past to wade through, but he's determined to help them through it as a family.

Eli learned early on to conform to the expectations put on him by his family. Doing anything else wouldn't be tolerated under any circumstances. When a stranger comes into his life sending it into a tailspin with a past he didn't remember.

He goes back to where it all started, a place he couldn't remember, only to find more questions than answers. As he unravels his memories, separating truth from nightmares, he wonders if he's doing more harm than good. But when he finds an ally from an unlikely source can he push past his own fears to be the person that was stripped from him?

NATE is an angst-ridden romance in the Single Dads of Gaynor Beach world with a man coming to terms with his past, a dad fighting for his kid and his business, and a family that is as accepting as it is unique.

Get it here: books2read.com/Nate

ALSO IN THE GAYNOR BEACH SERIES

AFTERWORD

Thank you so much for reading Jaime.

This sweet romance story has been lingering in my head for years. I'm so happy that I was finally able to bring it to life in this shared world. The Single Dads of Gaynor Beach has been a lovely project to be a part of. Sadly, this is my second and last book in the series, but I'm sure I'll be back for the spin-off!

To read my other Gaynor Beach book, check out Demetrius!

Books2read.com/demetrius

Also, don't forget to join my mailing list, for monthly book recs and updates. Here's the link.

http://eepurl.com/g-E50H

ABOUT THE AUTHOR

SA Sway is the contemporary pen name of author Sienna Sway.

When not writing, she can be found planning countless books and entertaining plot bunnies.

She is the mother to a loving toddler and partner to a lovely Irish man. She also lives in beautiful Coquitlam, BC in Canada, surrounded by mountains and forests.

She doesn't know how she got so lucky but is so grateful to her family and readers for supporting her dreams. She hopes to pay it forward.

Thank you for being here!

ALSO BY SA SWAY

Please note that all books can be read as standalones.